Cosmos Mindeleff

The Cliff Ruins of Canyon de Chelly, Arizona

Cosmos Mindeleff

The Cliff Ruins of Canyon de Chelly, Arizona

ISBN/EAN: 9783337387174

Printed in Europe, USA, Canada, Australia, Japan

Cover: Foto ©Andreas Hilbeck / pixelio.de

More available books at **www.hansebooks.com**

SIXTEENTH ANNUAL REPORT

OF THE

BUREAU OF AMERICAN ETHNOLOGY

TO THE

SECRETARY OF THE SMITHSONIAN INSTITUTION

1894-'95

BY

J. W. POWELL
DIRECTOR

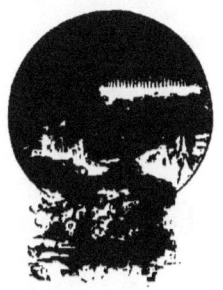

WASHINGTON
GOVERNMENT PRINTING OFFICE
1897

THE CLIFF RUINS

OF

CANYON DE CHELLY, ARIZONA

BY

COSMOS MINDELEFF

CONTENTS

ILLUSTRATIONS

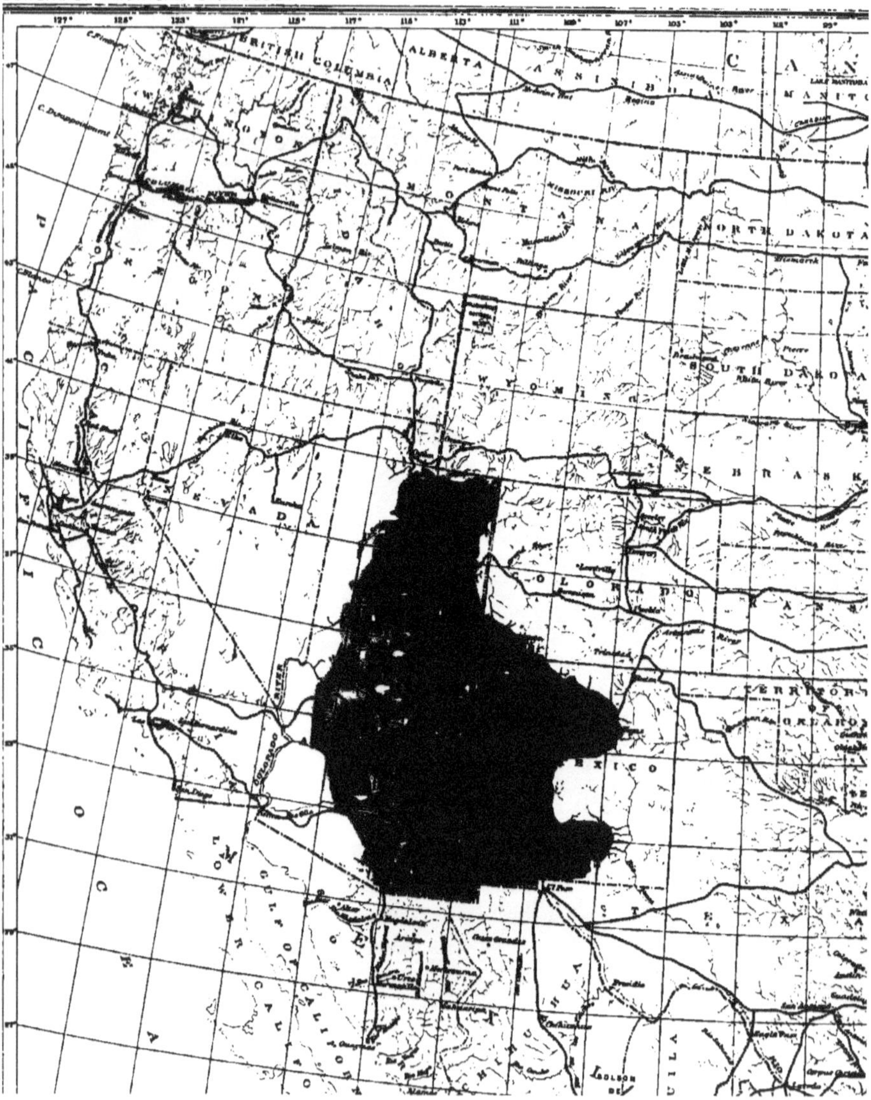
BRITISH COLUMBIA
ALBERTA
NORTH DAKOTA
SOUTH DAKOTA
NEVADA
COLORADO
GULF OF CALIFORNIA

ANCIENT PUEBLO REGION
SHOWING LOCATION OF
CANYON DE CHELLY

THE CLIFF RUINS OF CANYON DE CHELLY, ARIZONA

BY COSMOS MINDELEFF

INTRODUCTION

HISTORY AND LITERATURE

Although Canyon de Chelly is one of the best cliff-ruin regions of the United States, it is not easily accessible and is practically unknown. At the time of the conquest of this country by the "Army of the West" in 1846, and of the rush to California in 1849, vague rumors were current of wonderful "cities" built in the cliffs, but the position of the canyon in the heart of the Navaho country apparently prevented exploration. In 1849 it was found necessary to make a demonstration against these Indians, and an expedition was sent out under the command of Colonel Washington, then governor of New Mexico. A detachment of troops set out from Santa Fé, and was accompanied by Lieutenant (afterward General) J. H. Simpson, of the topographical engineers, to whose indefatigable zeal for investigation and carefulness of observation much credit is due. He was much interested in the archeology of the country passed over and his descriptions are remarkable for their freedom from the exaggerations and erroneous observations which characterize many of the publications of that period. His journal was published by Congress the next year[1] and was also printed privately.

The expedition camped in the Chin Lee valley outside of Canyon de Chelly, and Lieutenant Simpson made a side trip into the canyon itself. He mentions ruins noticed by him at 4½, 5, and 7 miles from the mouth; the latter, the ruin subsequently known as Casa Blanca, he describes at some length. He also gives an illustration drawn by R. H. Kern, which is very bad, and pictures some pottery fragments found near or in the ruin. The name De Chelly was apparently used before this time. Simpson obtained its orthography from Vigil, secretary of the province (of New Mexico), who told him it was of Indian origin and was pronounced *chay-e*. Possibly it was derived from the Navaho name of the place, Tsé-gi.

---

[1] Thirty-first Congress, first session, Senate Ex. Doc. No. 64, Washington, 1950.

Simpson's description, although very brief, formed the basis of all the succeeding accounts for the next thirty years. The Pacific railroad surveys, which added so much to our knowledge of the Southwest, did not touch this field. In 1860 the Abbé Domenech published his "Deserts of North America," which contains a reference to Casa Blanca ruin, but his knowledge was apparently derived wholly from Simpson. None of the assistants of the Hayden Survey actually penetrated the canyon, but one of them, W. H. Jackson, examined and described some ruins on the Rio de Chelly, in the lower Chin Lee valley. But in an article in Scribner's Magazine for December, 1878, Emma C. Hardacre published a number of descriptions and illustrations derived from the Hayden corps, among others figures one entitled "Ruins in Cañon de Chelly," from a drawing by Thomas Moran. The ruin can not be identified from the drawing.

This article is worth more than a passing notice, as it not only illustrates the extent of knowledge of the ruins at that time (1878), but probably had much to do with disseminating and making current erroneous inferences which survive to this day. In an introductory paragraph the author says:

Of late, blown over the plains, come stories of strange newly discovered cities of the far south-west; picturesque piles of masonry, of an age unknown to tradition. These ruins mark an era among antiquarians. The mysterious mound-builders fade into comparative insignificance before the grander and more ancient cliff-dwellers, whose castles lift their towers amid the sands of Arizona and crown the terraced slopes of the Rio Mancos and the Hovenweap.

Of the Chaco ruins it is said:

In size and grandeur of conception, they equal any of the present buildings of the United States, if we except the Capitol at Washington, and may without discredit be compared to the Pantheon and the Colosseum of the Old World.

In the same year Mr J. H. Beadle gave an account[1] of a visit he made to the canyon. He entered it over the Bat trail, near the junction of Monument canyon, and saw several ruins in the upper part. His descriptions are hardly more than a mention. Much archeologic data were secured by the assistants of the Wheeler Survey, but it does not appear that any of them, except the photographer, visited Canyon de Chelly. In the final reports of the Survey there is an illustration of the ruin visited by Lieutenant Simpson about thirty years before.[2] The illustration is a beautiful heliotype from a fine photograph made by T. H. O'Sullivan, but one serious defect renders it useless; through some blunder of the photographer or the engraver, the picture is reversed, the right and left sides being interchanged, so that to see it properly it must be looked at in a mirror. The illustration is accompanied by a short text, apparently prepared by Prof. F. W. Putnam, who edited the volume. The account by Simpson is quoted and some

[1] Western Wilds, and the Men who Redeem Them; Cincinnati, Philadelphia, Chicago, Memphis, 1878.
[2] U. S. Geog. Surveys West of the 100th Meridian, Lieutenant George M. Wheeler in charge; reports, vol. VII, Archæology; Washington, 1879, pp. 372-373, pl. XX.

additional data are given, derived from notes accompanying the photograph. The ruin is said to have "now received the name of the Casa Blanca, or White House," but the derivation of the name is not stated.

In 1882 Bancroft could find no better or fuller description than Simpson's, which he uses fully, and reproduces also Simpson's (Kern's) illustration. In the same year investigation by the assistants of the Bureau of Ethnology was commenced. Colonel James Stevenson and a party visited the canyon, and a considerable amount of data was obtained. In all, 46 ruins were visited, 17 of which were in Del Muerto; and sketches, ground plans, and photographs were obtained. The report of the Bureau for that year contains an account of this expedition, including a short description of a large ruin in Del Muerto, subsequently known as Mummy Cave. A brief account of the trip was also published elsewhere.[1] The next year a map of the canyon was made by the writer and many new ruins were discovered, making the total number in the canyon and its branches about 140. Since 1883 two short visits have been made to the place, the last late in 1893, and on each trip additional material was obtained. In 1890 Mr F. T. Bickford[2] published an account of a visit to the canyon, illustrated with a series of woodcuts made from the photographs of the Bureau. The illustrations are excellent and the text is pleasantly written, but the descriptions of ruins are too general to be of much value to the student.

In recent years several publications have appeared which, while not bearing directly on the De Chelly ruins, are of great interest, as they treat of analogous remains—the cliff ruins of the Mancos canyon and the Mesa Verde. These ruins were discovered in 1874 by W. H. Jackson and were visited and described in 1875 by W. H. Holmes,[3] both of the Hayden Survey. This region was roamed over by bands of renegade Ute and Navaho, who were constantly making trouble, and for fifteen years was apparently not visited by whites. Recent exploration appears to have been inaugurated by Mr F. H. Chapin, who spent two summers in the Mesa Verde country. Subsequently he published the results of some of his observations in a handsome little volume.[4] In 1891 Dr W. R. Birdsall made a flying trip to this region and published an account[5] of the ruins he saw the same year. At the time of this visit a more elaborate exploration was being carried on by the late G. Nordenskiöld, who made some excavations and obtained much valuable data which formed the basis of a book published in 1893.[6] This is the most important treatise on the cliff ruins that has ever been published, and the illustrations can only be characterized as magnificent. All of these works, and especially the last named, are of great value to the student of the cliff ruins wherever located, or of pueblo architecture.

[1] Bull. Am. Geog. Soc., 1886, No. 4; Ancient Habitations of the Southwest, by James Stevenson.
[2] Century Magazine, October, 1890, vol. xl., No. 6, p. 806 et seq.
[3] U. S. Geol. Survey, F. V. Hayden in charge; 10th Ann. Rept. (for 1876), Washington, 1878.
[4] The Land of the Cliff Dwellers, by Frederick H. Chapin; Boston, 1892.
[5] Bull. Am. Geog. Soc., vol. xxiii, No. 4, 1891; The Cliff Dwellings of the Cañons of the Mesa Verde.
[6] The Cliff Dwellers of the Mesa Verde, by G. Nordenskiöld; Stockholm and Chicago, 1894.

GEOGRAPHY

The ancient pueblo culture was so intimately connected with and
dependent on the character of the country where its remains are found
that some idea of this country is necessary to understand it. The limits
of the region are closely coincident with the boundaries of the plateau
country except on the south, so much so that a map of the latter,[1]
slightly extended around its margin, will serve to show the former.
The area of the ancient pueblo region may be 150,000 square miles;
that of the plateau country, approximately, 130,000.

The plateau country is not a smooth and level region, as its name
might imply; it is extremely rugged, and the topographic obstacles to
travel are greater than in many wild mountain regions. It is a country of cliffs and canyons, often of considerable magnitude and forming
a bar to extended progress in any direction. The surface is generally
smooth or slightly undulating and apparently level, but it is composed
of a series of platforms or mesas, which are seldom of great extent
and generally terminate at the brink of a wall, often of huge dimensions. There are mesas everywhere; it is the mesa country.

Although the strata appear to be horizontal, they are slightly tilted.
The inclination, although slight, is remarkably persistent, and the
thickness of the strata remains almost constant. The beds, therefore,
extend from very high altitudes to very low ones, and often the formation which is exposed to view at the summit of an incline is lost to
view after a few miles, being covered by some later formation, which
in turn is covered by a still later one. Each formation thus appears
as a terrace, bounded on one side by a descending cliff carved out of
the edges of its own strata and on the other by an ascending cliff
carved out of the strata which overlie it. This is the more common
form, although isolated mesas, bits of tableland completely engirdled
by cliffs, are but little less common.

The courses of the margins of the mesas are not regular. The cliffs
sometimes maintain an average trend through great distances, but in
detail their courses are extremely crooked; they wind in and out, forming alternate alcoves and promontories in the wall, and frequently they
are cut through by valleys, which may be either narrow canyons or
interspaces 10 or even 20 miles wide.

The whole region has been subjected to many displacements, both
flexures of the monoclinal type and faults. Some of these flexures
attain a length of over 80 miles and a displacement of 3,000 feet, and the
faults reach even a greater magnitude. There is also an abundance of
volcanic rocks and extinct volcanoes, and while the principal eruptions
have occurred about the borders of the region, extending but slightly

---

[1] See Major C. E. Dutton's map of the plateau country in 6th Ann. Rept. U. S. Geol. Survey, pl. xi.
His report on "Mount Taylor and the Zuñi plateau," of which this map is a part, presents a vivid
picture of the plateau country, and his descriptions are so clear and expressive that any attempt to
better them must result in failure. The statement of the geologic and topographic features which is
incorporated herein is derived directly from Major Dutton's description, much of it being taken bodily.

into it, traces of lesser disturbances can be found throughout the country. It has been said that if a geologist should actually make the circuit of the plateau country, he could so conduct his route that for three-fourths of the time he would be treading upon volcanic materials and could pitch his camp upon them every night. The oldest eruptions do not go back of Tertiary time, while some are so recent as probably to come within the historic period—within three or four centuries.

The strata of the plateau country are remarkable for their homogeneity, when considered with reference to their horizontal extensions; hardly less so for their diversity when considered in their vertical relation. Although the groups differ radically from each other, still each preserves its characteristics with singularly slight degrees of variation from place to place. Hence we have a certain amount of similarity and monotony in the landscape which is aided rather than diminished by the vegetation; for the vegetation, like the human occupants of this country, has come under its overpowering influence. The characteristic landscape consists of a wide expanse of featureless plains, bounded by far-off cliffs in gorgeous colors; in the foreground a soil of bright yellow or ashy gray; over all the most brilliant sunlight, while the distant features are softened by a blue haze.

The most conspicuous formation of the whole region is a massive bright-red sandstone out of which have been carved "the most striking and typical features of those marvelous plateau landscapes which will be subjects of wonder and delight to all coming generations of men. The most superb canyons of the neighboring region, the Canyon de Chelly and the Del Muerto, the lofty pinnacles and towers of the San Juan country, the finest walls in the great upper chasms of the Colorado, are the vertical edges of this red sandstone."

Of the climate of the plateau country it has been said that in the large valleys it is "temperate in winter and insufferable in summer; higher up the summers are temperate and the winters barely sufferable." It is as though there were two distinct regions covering the same area, for there are marked differences throughout, except in topographic configuration, between the lowlands and the uplands or high plateaus. The lowlands present an appearance which is barren and desolate in the extreme, although the soil is fertile and under irrigation yields good crops. Vegetation is limited to a scanty growth of grass during a small part of the year, with small areas here and there scantily covered by the prickly greasewood and at intervals by clumps of sagebrush; but even these prefer a higher level, and develop better on the neighboring mesas than in the valleys proper. The arborescent growth consists of sparsely distributed cottonwoods and willows, closely confined to the river bottoms. On intermediate higher levels junipers and cedars appear, often standing so closely together as to seriously impede travel, but they are confined to the tops of mesas and other high ground, the valleys being generally clear or covered with sagebrush. Still higher up yellow pines become abundant and in places spread out into magnificent forests, while in some mountain regions scrub oak, quaking asp, and even spruce trees are abundant.

In the mountain regions there is often a reasonable amount of moisture, and some crops, potatoes for example, are grown there without irrigation; but the season is short. In the Tunicha mountains the Navaho raise corn at an altitude of nearly 8,000 feet, but they often lose the crop from drought or from frost. On the intermediate levels and in the lowlands cultivation by modern methods is practically impossible without irrigation, except in a few favored localities, where a crop can be obtained perhaps two years or three years in five. But with a minute knowledge of the climatic conditions, and with methods adapted to meet these conditions, scanty crops can be and are raised by the Indians without irrigation throughout the whole region; but everywhere that water can be applied the product of the soil is increased many fold.

Near the center of the plateau country, in the northeastern corner of Arizona, a range of mountains crosses diagonally from northwest to southeast, extending into New Mexico. In the north an irregular cluster of considerable size, separated from the remainder of the range, is called the Carrizo; and the range proper has no less than three names applied to different parts of it. The northern end is known as the Lukachukai, the central part as the Tunicha, and the southern part as the Chuska or Choiskai mountains, all Navaho names. The two former clusters attain an altitude of 9,500 feet; the Tunicha and the Chuska are about 9,000 feet high, the latter having a flat top of considerable area.

On the east these mountains break down rather abruptly into the broad valley of the Chaco river, or the Chaco wash, as it is more commonly designated; on the west they break down gradually, through a series of slopes and mesas, into the Chin Lee valley. Canyon de Chelly has been cut in the western slope by a series of small streams, which, rising near the crest of the mountain, combine near its head and flow in a general westerly direction. The mouth of the canyon is on the eastern border of the Chin Lee valley. It is 60 miles south of the Utah boundary and 25 miles west of that of New Mexico; hence it is 60 miles east and a little north from the old province of Tusayan, the modern Moki, and 85 miles northwest from the old province of Cibola, the modern Zuñi. Its position is almost in the heart of the ancient pueblo region; the Chaco ruins lie about 80 miles east, and the ruins of the San Juan from 60 to 80 miles north and northeast.

The geographic position of Canyon de Chelly has had an important effect on its history, forming as it does an available resting place in any migratory movement either on the north and south line or east and west. The Tunicha mountains are a serious obstacle to north and

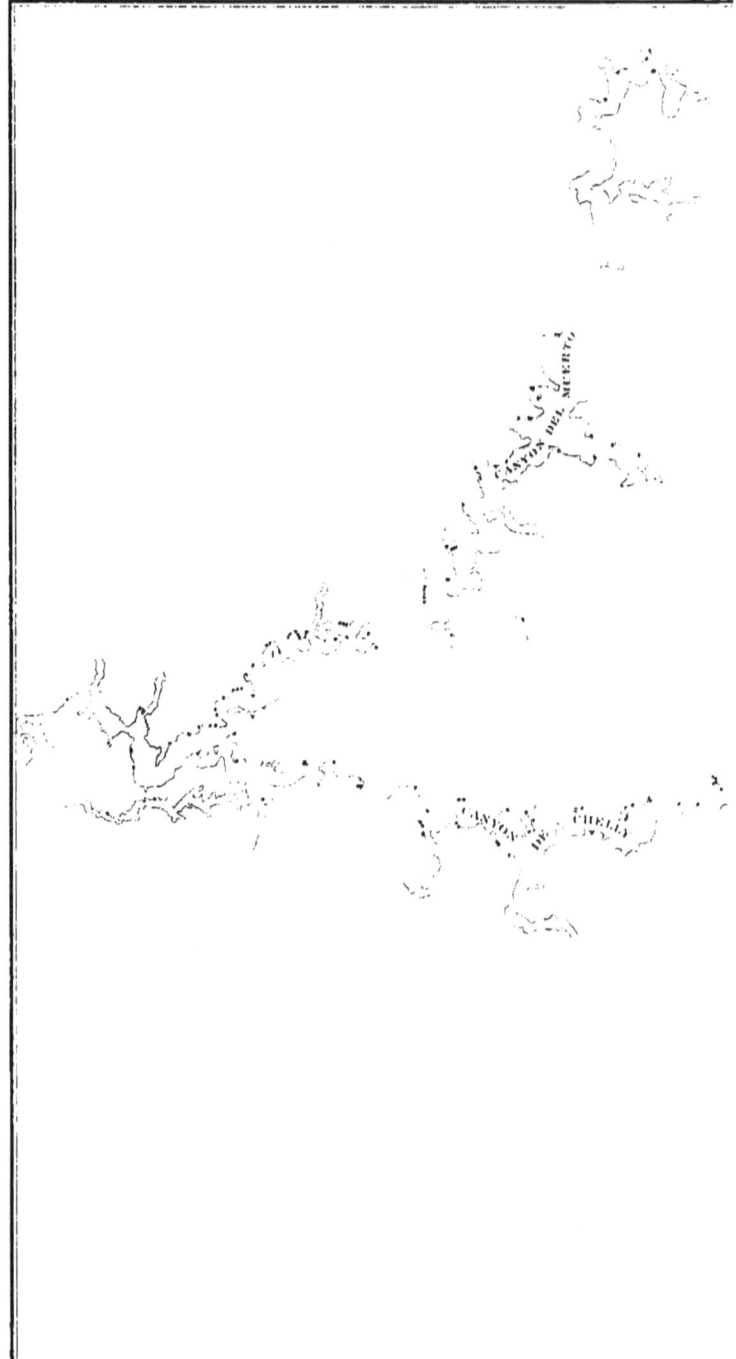

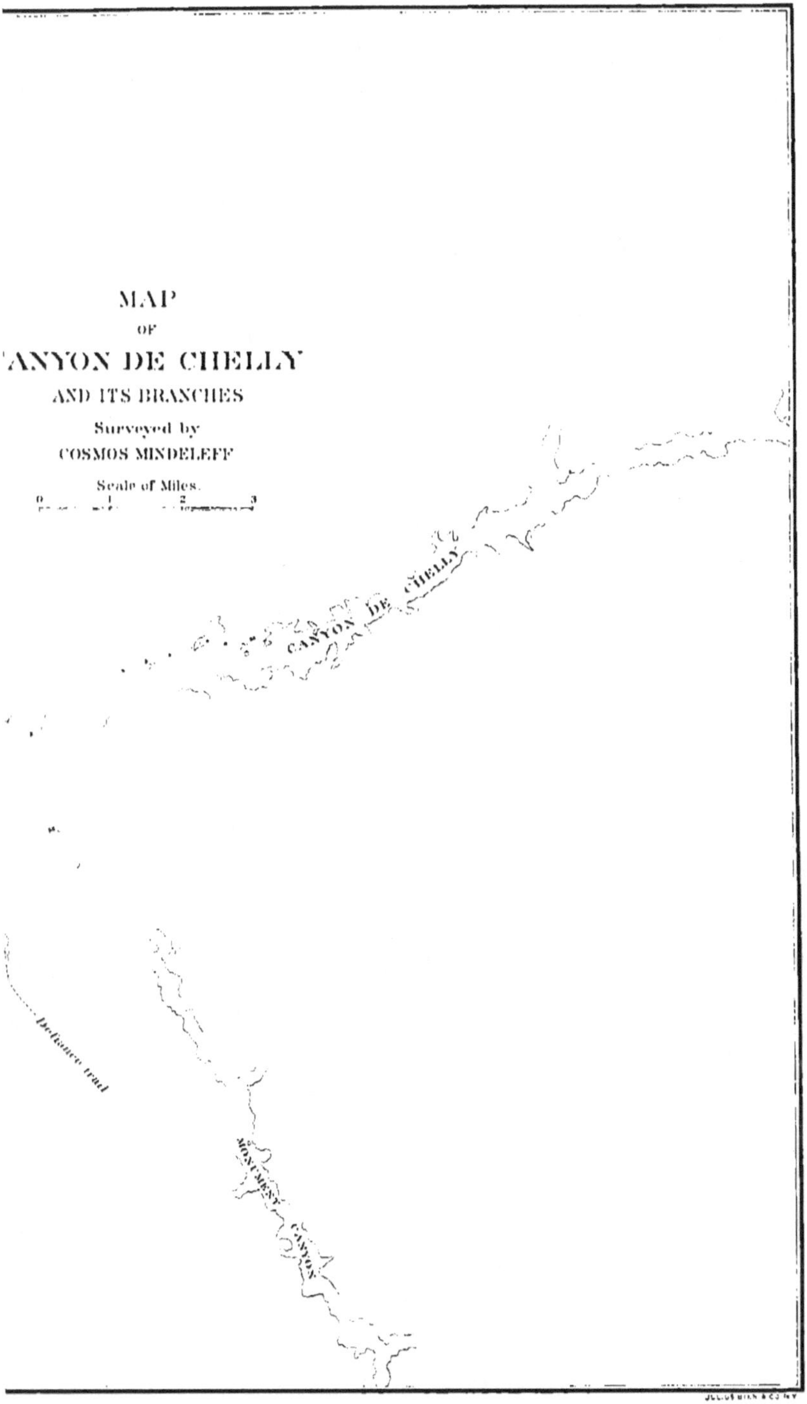

MAP

OF

ANYON DE CHELLY

AND ITS BRANCHES

Surveyed by

COSMOS MINDELEFF

Scale of Miles.

0   1   2   3

CANYON DE CHELLY

CANYON DE CHELLY

Defiance trail

MONUMENT CANYON

south movement at the present day, but less so than the arid valleys which border them. Except at one place, and that place is difficult, it is almost impossible to cross the mountains with a wheeled vehicle, but there are innumerable trails running in all directions, and these trails are in constant use by the Navaho, except in the depths of winter. The mountain route is preferable, however, to the valley roads, where the traveler for several days is without wood, with very little water and forage, and his movements are impeded by deep sand.

To the traveler on foot, or even on horseback, Canyon de Chelly is easily accessible from almost any direction. Good trails run northward to the San Juan and northeastward over the Tunicha mountains to the upper part of that river; Fort Defiance is but half a day's journey to the southeast; Tusayan and Zuñi are but three days distant to the traveler on foot; the Navaho often ride the distance in a day or a day and a half. The canyon is accessible to wagons, however, only at its mouth.

The main canyon, shown on the map (plate XLII) as Canyon de Chelly and known to the Navaho as Tsé-gi, is about 20 miles long. It heads near Washington pass, within a few miles of the crest of the mountain, and extends almost due west to the Chin Lee valley. The country descends by a regular slope from an altitude of about 7,500 feet at the foot of the main crest to about 5,200 feet in the Chin Lee valley, 25 miles west, and is so much cut up locally by ravines and washes that it is impassable to wagons, but it preserves throughout its mesa-like character.

About 3 miles from its mouth De Chelly is joined by another canyon almost as long, which, heading also in the Tunicha mountains, comes in from the northeast. It is over 15 miles long, and is called on the map Canyon del Muerto; the Navaho know it as Én-a-tsé-gi. About 13 miles above the mouth of the main canyon a small branch comes in from the southeast. It is about 10 miles long, and has been called Monument canyon, on account of the number of upright natural pinnacles of rock in it. In addition to those named there are innumerable small branches, ranging in size from deep coves to real canyons a mile or two long. Outside of De Chelly, and independent of it, there is a little canyon about 4 miles long, called Tse-on-i-tso-si by the Navaho. At one point near its head it approaches so near to De Chelly that but a few feet of rock separate them.

On the western side of the mountains there are a number of small perennial streams fed by springs on the upper slopes. Several of these meet in the upper part of De Chelly, others in Del Muerto, and in the upper parts of these canyons there is generally water. But, except at the time of the autumn and winter rains and in the spring when the mountain snows are melting, the streams are not powerful enough to carry the water to the mouth of the canyon. The flow is absorbed by the deep sand which forms the stream bed. Ordinarily it is difficult to procure enough water to drink less than 8 or 10 miles from the mouth of De Chelly, but occasionally the whole stream bed, at places over a quarter of a mile wide, is occupied by a raging torrent impassable to man or beast. Such ebullitions, however, seldom last more than a few hours. Usually water can be obtained anywhere in the bottom by sinking a shallow well in the sand, and it is by this method that the Navaho, the present occupants of the canyon, obtain their supply.

The walls of the canyon are composed of brilliant red sandstone, discolored everywhere by long streaks of black and gray coming from above. At its mouth it is about 500 feet wide. Higher up the walls sometimes approach to 300 feet of each other, elsewhere broadening out to half a mile or more; but everywhere the wall line is tortuous and crooked in the extreme, and, while the general direction of De Chelly is east and west, the traveler on the trail which runs through it is as often headed north or south. Del Muerto is even more tortuous than De Chelly, and in places it is so narrow that one could almost throw a stone across it.

At its mouth the walls of Canyon de Chelly are but 20 to 30 feet high, descending vertically to a wide bed of loose white sand, and absolutely free from talus or débris. Three miles above Del Muerto comes in, but its mouth is so narrow it appears like an alcove and might easily be overlooked. Here the walls are over 200 feet high, but the rise is so gradual that it is impossible to appreciate its amount. At the point where Monument canyon comes in, 13 miles above the mouth of De Chelly, the walls reach a height of over 800 feet, about one-third of which consists of talus.

The rise in the height of the walls is so gradual that when the canyon is entered at its mouth the mental scale by which we estimate distances and magnitudes is lost and the wildest conjectures result. We fail at first to realize the stupendous scale on which the work was done, and when we do finally realize it we swing to the opposite side and exaggerate. At the junction of Monument canyon there is a beautiful rock pinnacle or needle standing out clear from the cliff and not more than 165 feet on the ground. It has been named, in conjunction with a somewhat similar pinnacle on the other side of the canyon, "The Captains," and its height has been variously estimated at from 1,200 to 2,500 feet. It is less than 800. A curious illustration of the effects of the scenery in connection with this pinnacle may not be amiss. The author of Western Wilds (Cincinnati, 1878) thus describes it:

But the most remarkable and unaccountable feature of the locality is where the canyons meet. There stands out 100 feet from the point, entirely isolated, a vast leaning rock tower at least 1,200 feet high and not over 200 thick at the base, as if it had originally been the sharp termination of the cliff and been broken off and shoved farther out. It almost seems that one must be mistaken; that it must have some connection with the cliff, until one goes around it and finds it 100 feet or more from the former. It leans at an angle from the perpendicular of at least 15 degrees; and lying down at the base on the under side, by the best sighting I could make, it seemed to me that the opposite upper edge was directly over me—that is to say, mechanically speaking, its center of gravity barely falls with the base, and a heave of only a yard or two more would cause it to topple over. (Page 257.)

The dimensions have already been given. The pinnacle is perfectly plumb.

The rock of which the canyon walls are formed is a massive sandstone in which the lines of bedding are almost completely obliterated. It is rather soft in texture, and has been carved by atmospheric erosion into grotesque and sometimes beautiful forms. In places great blocks have fallen off, leaving smooth vertical surfaces, extending sometimes from the top nearly to the stream bed, 400 feet or more in height and as much in breadth. In the lower parts of the canyons the walls, sometimes of the character described, sometimes with the surfaces and angles smoothed by the flying sand, are generally vertical and often overhang, descending sheer to the canyon bottom without talus or intervening slopes of débris. The talus, where there is any, is slight and consists of massive sandstone of the same character as the walls, but much rounded by atmospheric erosion. The enlarged map (plate XLIII) shows something of this character.

Near its mouth the whole bottom of the canyon consists of an even stretch of white sand extending from cliff to cliff. A little higher up there are small areas of alluvium, or bottom land, in recesses and coves in the walls and generally only a foot or two above the stream bed. Still higher up these areas become more abundant and of greater extent, forming regular benches or terraces, generally well raised above the stream bed. At the Casa Blanca ruin, 7 miles up the canyon, the bench is 8 or 10 feet above the stream. Each little branch canyon and deep cove in the cliffs is fronted by a more or less extended area of this cultivable bottom land. Ten miles up the talus has become a prominent feature. It consists of broken rock, sand, and soil, generally overlying a slope of massive sandstone, such as has been described, and which occasionally crops out on the surface. With the development of the talus the area of bottom land dwindles, and the former encroaches more and more until a little above the junction of Monument canyon the bottom land is limited to narrow strips and small patches here and there.

These bottom lands are the cultivable areas of the canyon bottom, and their occurrence and distribution have dictated the location of the villages now in ruins. They are also the sites of all the Navaho settlements in the canyon. The Navaho hogans are generally placed directly on the bottoms; the ruins are always so located as to overlook them. Only a very small proportion of the available land is utilized by the Navaho, and not all of it was used by the old village builders. The Navaho sites, as a whole, are far superior to the village sites.

The horticultural conditions here, while essentially the same as those of the whole pueblo region, present some peculiar features. Except for a few modern examples there are no traces of irrigating works, and the Navaho work can not be regarded as a success. The village builders probably did not require irrigation for the successful cultivation of their crops, and under the ordinary Indian methods of planting and cultivation a failure to harvest a good crop was probably rare. After the harvest season it is the practice of the Navaho to abandon the canyon for the winter, driving their flocks and carrying the season's produce to more open localities in the neighboring valleys. The canyon is not a desirable place of residence in the winter to a people who live in the saddle and have large flocks of sheep and goats, but there is no evidence that the old inhabitants followed the Navaho practice.

During most of the year there is no water in the lower 10 miles of the canyons, where most of the cultivable land is situated. The autumn rains in the mountains, which occur late in July or early in August, sometimes send down a little stream, which, however, generally lasts but a few days and fails to reach the mouth of the canyon. Late in October, or early in November, a small amount comes down and is fairly permanent through the winter and spring. The stream bed is even more tortuous than the canyon it occupies, often washing the cliffs on one side, then passing directly across the bottom and returning again to the same side, the stream bed being many times wider than the stream, which constantly shifts its channel. In December it becomes very cold and so much of the stream is in shade during a large part of the day that much of the water becomes frozen and, as it were, held in place. In the warm parts of the day, and in the sunshine, the ice is melted, the stream resumes its flow, and so gradually pushes its way farther and farther down the canyon. But some sections, less exposed to warmth than others, retain their ice during the day. These points are flooded by the water from above, which is again frozen during the night and again flooded the next day, and so on. In a short time great fields of smooth ice are formed, which render travel on horseback very difficult and even dangerous. This, and the scant grazing afforded by the bottom lands in winter, doubtless is the cause of the annual migration of the Navaho; but these conditions would not materially affect a people living in the canyon who did not possess or were but scantily supplied with horses and sheep. The stream when it is flowing is seldom more than a foot deep, generally only a few inches, except in times of flood, when it becomes a raging torrent, carrying everything before it. Hence irrigation would be impracticable, even if its principles were known, nor is it essential here to successful horticulture.

One of the characteristic features of the canyons at the present day is the immense number of peach trees within them. Wherever there is a favorable site, in some sheltered cove or little branch canyon, there is a clump of peach trees, in some instances perhaps as many as 1,000 in one "orchard." When the peaches ripen, hundreds and even thousands of Navaho flock to the place, coming from all over the reservation, like an immense flock of vultures, and with disastrous results to the food supply. A few months after it is difficult to procure even a handful of dried fruit. The peach trees are, of course, modern. They were introduced into this country originally by the Spanish monks, but in De Chelly there are not more than two or three

trees which are older than the last Navaho war. At that time, it is
said, the soldiers cut down every peach tree they could find. But,
aside from the peaches, De Chelly was until recently the great agricultural center of the Navaho tribe, and large quantities of corn, mel-
ons, pumpkins, beans, etc. were and are raised there every year.
Under modern conditions many other localities now vie with it, and
some surpass it in output of agricultural products, but not many years
ago De Chelly was regarded as the place par excellence.

It will be clear, therefore, that prior to very recent times De Chelly
would be selected by almost any tribe moving across the country, and,
barring a hostile prior occupancy, would be the most desirable place
for the pursuit of horticultural operations for many miles in any direction. The vicinity of the Tunicha mountains, which could be reached
in half a day from any part of the canyons, and which must have
abounded in game, for even now some is found there, would be a
material advantage. The position of the canyon in the heart of the
plateau country and of the ancient pueblo region would make it a
natural stopping place during any migratory movement either north
and south or east and west, and its settlement was doubtless due to
this favorable position and to the natural advantages it offered. This
settlement was effected probably not by one band or tribe, nor at one
time, but by many bands at many times. Probably the first settlements were very old; certainly the last were very recent.

CLASSIFICATION AND DESCRIPTIONS

RUINS OF THE PUEBLO REGION

No satisfactory general classification of the ruins of the ancient
pueblo region has yet been made; possibly because the material in
hand is not sufficiently abundant. There are thousands of ruins scattered over the southwest, of many different types which merge more
or less into each other. In 1884 Mr A. F. Bandelier, whose knowledge
of the archeology of the southwest is very extensive, formulated a
classification, and in 1892, in his final report,[1] he announces that he
has nothing to change in it. The classification is as follows:

I. Large communal houses several stories high.
> (a) Composed of one or two, seldom three, extensive buildings, generally
> so disposed as to surround an interior court.
> (b) Polygonal pueblos.
> (c) Scattered pueblos, composed of a number of large many-storied houses,
> disposed in a more or less irregular manner; sometimes in irregular
> squares or on a line.
> (d) Artificial caves, resembling in number, size, and disposition of the
> cells the many-storied communal dwelling.
> (e) Many-storied dwellings, with artificial walls, erected inside of natural
> caves of great size.

II. Detached family dwellings, either isolated or in groups forming villages.

---

[1] Arch. Inst. of America, 5th Ann. Rept., p. 55; and Arch. Inst. of America, Papers, American series,
IV, p. 27.

Many hundreds of ruins have been examined by Mr. Bandelier, and doubtless the classification above afforded a convenient working basis for the region with which he is most familiar, the basin of the Rio Grande and its tributaries. It does not apply very well to the western part of the pueblo region.

The distinguishing characteristics of the first group (of five classes)—houses several stories high—are as follows: Each building consisted of an agglomeration of a great number of small cells, without any larger halls of particularly striking dimensions. 'All the buildings, except outhouses or additions, were at least two stories high, and the lower story was entered only from the roof. The various stories receded from the bottom to the top. The prevalence of the estufa (kiva) generally, or often, circular in form.

Ruins of class II—detached family dwellings—consist sometimes of a single room; more often of several rooms. The rooms are generally built of stone, although examples constructed of mud and adobe are also found in certain regions. The average size of the room is larger than in the communal building, and there is a gradual increase in size of rooms from north to south. There are front doorways and light and air holes are larger than in the communal houses. Mr Bandelier suggests that the detached family dwelling was the early type, and that only when enemies began to threaten were the communal houses resorted to for purposes of defense.

This classification is apparently based on external form alone, without taking into account the numerous influences which modify or produce form; and while no doubt it was sufficient for field use, it is not likely to be permanently adopted; for there does not appear to be any essential or radical difference between the various classes. Moreover, there does not appear to be any place in the scheme for the cliff ruins of the variety especially abundant in De Chelly and found in many other localities, unless indeed such ruins come under class II—detached family dwellings; yet this would imply precedence in time, and the ruins themselves will not permit such an inference.

The essential uniformity of types which prevails over the immense area covered by the ancient pueblo ruins is a noteworthy feature, and any system of classification which does not take it into account must be considered as only tentative. What elements should be considered and what weight assigned to each in preparing a scheme of classification is yet to be determined, but probably one of the most important elements is the character of the site occupied, with reference to its convenience and defensibility. There are great differences in kind between the great valley pueblos, located without reference to defense and depending for security on their size and the number of their population, of which Zuñi and Taos are examples, and the villages which are located on high mesas and projecting tongues of rock; in other words, on defensive sites where reliance for security was placed on the char-

acter of the site occupied, such as the Tusayan villages of today.
Within each of these classes there are varieties, and there are also
secondary types which pertain sometimes to one, sometimes to the
other, and sometimes to both. Such are the cliff ruins, the cavate
lodges, and the single house remains.

The unit of pueblo architecture is the single cell, and in its development the highest point reached is the aggregation of a great number
of such cells into one or more clusters, either connected with or adjacent
to each other. These cells were all the same, or essentially so; for while
differentiation in use or function had been or was being developed at
the time of the Spanish conquest, differentiation in form had not been
reached. The kiva, of circular or rectangular shape, is a survival and
not a development.

Large aggregations of many cells into one cluster are the latest
development of pueblo architecture. They were immediately preceded
by a type composed of a larger number of smaller villages, located on
sites selected with reference to their ease of defense, and apparently
the change from the latter to the former type was made at one step,
without developing any intermediate forms. The differences between
the largest examples of villages on defensive sites and the smallest
appear to be only differences of size. Doubtless in the early days of
pueblo architecture small settlements were the rule. Probably these
settlements were located in the valleys, on sites most convenient for
horticulture, each gens occupying its own village. Incursions by neighboring wild tribes, or by hostile neighbors, and constant annoyance
and loss at their hands, gradually compelled the removal of these little
villages to sites more easily defended, and also forced the aggregation
of various related gentes into one group or village. At a still later
period the same motive, considerably emphasized perhaps, compelled
a further removal to even more difficult sites. The Tusayan villages
at the time of the Spanish discovery were located on the foothills of
the mesas, and many pueblo villages at that period occupied similar
sites. Actuated by fear of the Ute and Comanche, and perhaps of
the Spaniards, the inhabitants soon after moved to the top of the
mesa, where they now are. Many villages stopped at this stage. Some
were in this stage at the time of the discovery—Acoma, for example.
Finally, whole villages whose inhabitants spoke the same language
combined to form one larger village, which, depending now on size
and numbers for defense, was again located on a site convenient for
horticulture.

The process sketched above was by no means continuous. The population was in slow but practically constant movement, much the same
as that now taking place in the Zuñi country; it was a slow migration.
Outlying settlements were established at points convenient to cultivable fields, and probably were intended to be occupied only during the
summer. Sometimes these temporary sites might be found more convenient than that of the parent village, and it would gradually come

about that some of the inhabitants would remain there all the year. Eventually the temporary settlement might outgrow the parent, and would in turn put out other temporary settlements. This process would be possible only during prolonged periods of peace, but it is known to have taken place in several regions. Necessarily hundreds of small settlements, ranging in size from one room to a great many, would be established, and as the population moved onward would be abandoned, without ever developing into regular villages occupied all the year. It is believed that many of the single house remains of Mr Bandelier's classification[1] belong to this type, as do also many cavate lodges, and in the present paper it will be shown that some at least of the cliff ruins belong to the same category.

The cliff ruins are a striking feature, and the ordinary traveler is apt to overlook the more important ruins which sometimes, if not generally, are associated with them. The study of the ruins in Canyon de Chelly has led to the conclusion that the cliff ruins there are generally subordinate structures, connected with and inhabited at the same time as a number of larger home villages located on the canyon bottom, and occupying much the same relation to the latter that Moen-kapi does to Oraibi, or that Nutria, Pescado, and Ojo Caliente do to Zuñi; and that they are the functional analogues of the "watch towers" of the San Juan and of Zuñi, and the brush shelters or "kisis" of Tusayan; in other words, they were horticultural outlooks occupied only during the farming season.

Mr G. Nordenskiöld, who examined a number of cliff and other ruins in the Mancos canyon and the Mesa Verde region, adopts[2] a very simple classification, as follows:

I. Ruins in the valleys, on the plains, or on the plateaus.
II. Ruins in caves in the walls of the canyons, subdivided as follows:
    (a) Cave dwellings, or caves inhabited without the erection of any buildings within them.
    (b) Cliff dwellings, or buildings erected in caves.

From its topographic character it might be expected that the Canyon de Chelly ruins would hardly come within a scheme of classification based upon those found in the open country; and here, if anywhere, we should find corroboration of the old idea that the cliff ruins were the homes and last refuge of a race harassed by powerful enemies and finally driven to the construction of dwellings in inaccessible cliffs, where a last ineffectual stand was made against their foes; or the more recent theory that they represent an early stage in the development of pueblo architecture, when the pueblo builders were few in number and surrounded by numerous enemies. Neither of these theories are in accord with the facts of observation. The still later idea that the cliff dwellings were used as places of refuge by various pueblo tribes who, when

---

[1] See a paper by the author on "Aboriginal remains in Verde valley, Arizona," in 13th Ann. Rept. Bureau of Ethnology, p. 179 et seq.
[2] The Cliff Dwellers of the Mesa Verde, pp. 9 and 114.

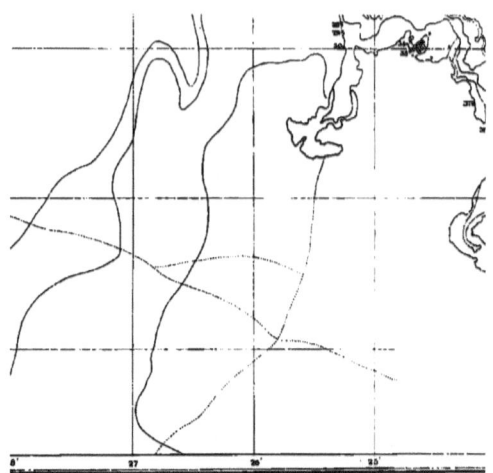

DETAILED MAP OF PART OF CANYON DE CHELLY SHOWING

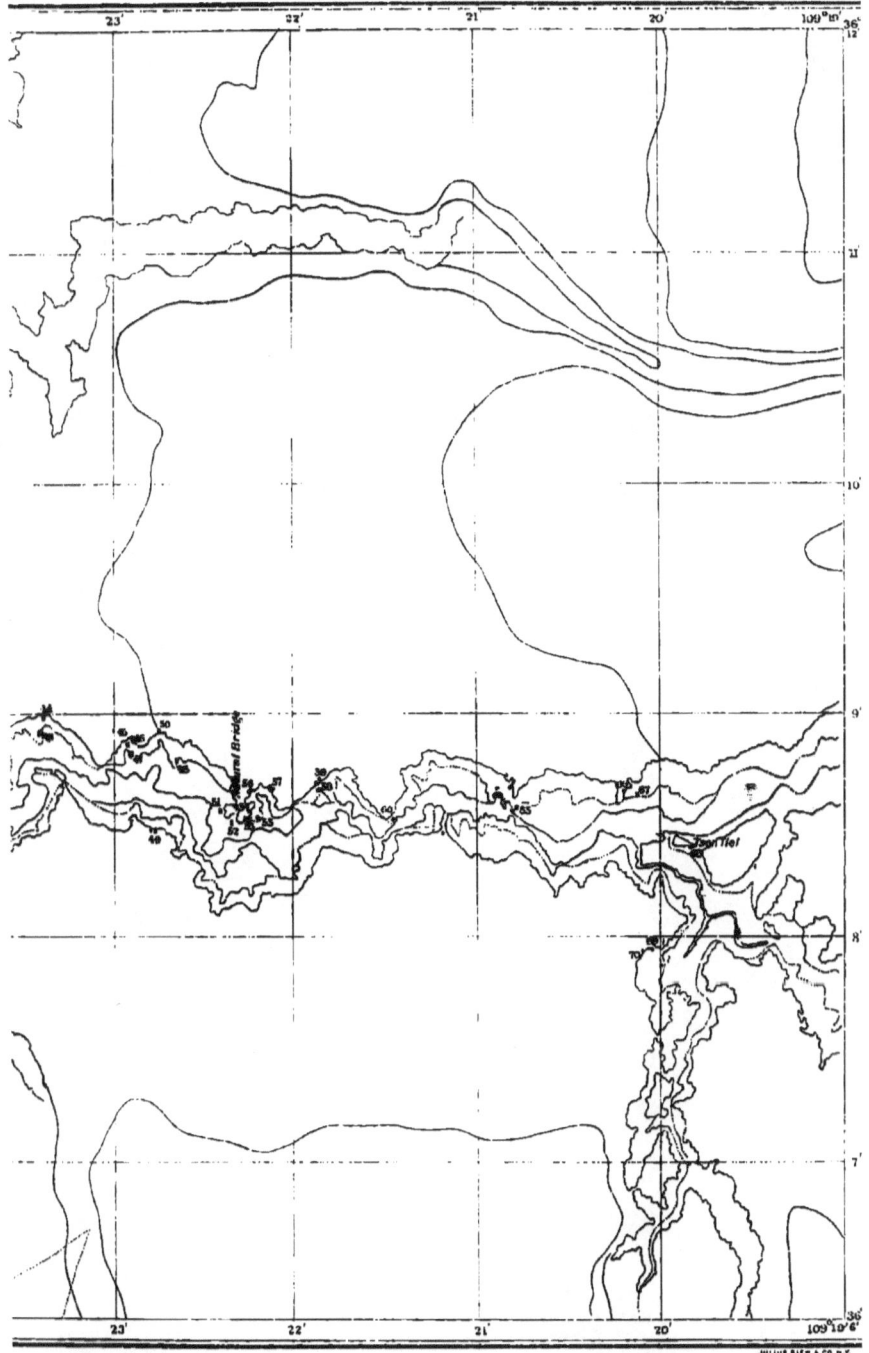

OF CULTIVABLE LAND

the occasion for such use was passed, returned to their original homes, or to others constructed like them, may explain some of the cliff ruins, but if applicable at all to those of De Chelly, it applies only to a small number of them.

The ruins of De Chelly show unmistakably several periods of occupancy, extending over considerable time and each fairly complete. They fall easily into the classification previously suggested, and exhibit various types, but the earliest and the latest forms are not found. In the descriptions which follow the classification below has been employed:

     I—Old villages on open sites.
     II—Home villages on bottom lands.
     III—Home villages located for defense.
     IV Cliff outlooks or farming shelters.

I—OLD VILLAGES ON OPEN SITES

In the upper part of the canyon, and extending into what we may call the middle region, there are a number of ruins that seem to be out of place in this locality. They are exactly similar to hundreds of ruins found in the open country; such, for example, as the older villages of Tusayan, located on low foothills at the foot of the mesa, and the peculiar topographic characteristics of the location have not made the slightest impression on them. These ruins are located on gentle slopes, the foothills of the talus, as it were, away from the cliffs, and are now marked only by scattered fragments of building stone and broken pottery. The ground plans are in all cases indistinguishable; in only a few instances can even a short wall line be traced. They seem to have been located without special reference to large areas of cultivable land, although they always command small areas of such land. There is a remarkable uniformity in ruins of this type in character of site occupied, outlook, and general appearance. They are always close to the stream bed, seldom more than 10 or 12 feet above it, and the sites were chosen apparently without any reference to their defensibility. A typical example occurs at the point marked 60 on the detailed map (plate XLIII), another occurs at 58, and another at 52. One of the largest examples is in the lower part of the canyon. At the junction of Del Muerto there is a large mass of rock standing out alone and extending nearly to the full height of the canyon walls. On the south it is connected with the main wall back of it by a low tongue of rock, sparsely covered in places by soil and sand, and on the top of this tongue or saddle there is a large ruin of the type described, but no ground plan can now be made out. Possibly the obliterated appearance of this ruin and of others of the same class is due to the use of the material, ready to hand and of the proper size, in later structures. It is known that a similar appearance was produced in Tusayan by such a cause. The old village of Walpi, on a foothill below the mesa point and the site of the village at the time of the Spanish conquest, presents an appearance of great antiquity, although it was partly occupied so late as fifty years ago. When the movement to the summit of the mesa became general, the material of the old houses was utilized in the construction of the new ones, and at the present day it can almost be said that not one stone remains above another. So complete is the obliteration that no ground plan can be made out.

If similar conditions prevailed in De Chelly, there might be many more ruins of this class than those so far discovered. Even those found are not easily distinguished and might easily be passed over. Possibly there were small ruins of this type scattered over the whole canyon bottom. An example which occurs at the point marked 12 on the map, and shown in plate XLIV, presents no trace on the surface except some potsherds, which in this locality mean nothing. The site is a low hill or end of a slope, the top of which is perhaps 25 feet above the stream bed, but separated from it by a belt of recent alluvium carpeted with grass. The hill itself was formed of talus, covered with alluvium, all but a small portion of which was subsequently cut away, leaving an almost vertical face 15 or 18 feet high. In this face the ends or vertical sections of several walls can be seen; one of them is nearly 3 feet thick and extends 4 feet below the present ground surface.

The filling of these ruins to a depth of 4 or 5 feet and the almost complete absence of surface remains or indications does not necessarily imply a remote antiquity, although it suggests it. During the fall and early winter months tremendous sand storms rage in the canyon; the wind sweeps through the gorge with an almost irresistible power, carrying with it such immense quantities of sand that objects a few hundred feet distant can not be distinguished. These sand storms were and are potent factors in producing the picturesque features of the red cliffs forming the canyon walls; but they are constructive as well as destructive, and cavities and hollow places in exposed situations such as the canyon bottom are soon filled up. The stream itself is also a powerful agent of destruction and construction; during flood periods banks of sand and alluvium are often cut away and sometimes others are formed. Yet there are reasons for believing that the old village ruins on open sites, now almost obliterated, mark the first period in the occupancy of the canyon, perhaps even a period distinctly separated from the others. Excavation on these sites would probably yield valuable results.

II—HOME VILLAGES ON BOTTOM LANDS

Ruins comprised in the second class are located on the bottom lands, generally at the base of a cliff, and without reference to the defensibility of the site. They are, as a rule, much broken down, and might perhaps be classed with the ruins already described, but there are some distinctive features which justify us in separating them. Ruins of this class are always located either at the base of a cliff or in a cove under it, on the level or raised but slightly above the bottom land, and sometimes at a considerable distance from the stream. The ground plans

SECTION OF OLD WALLS, CANYON DE CHELLY

can generally be distinguished, and in many instances walls are still standing—sometimes to a height of three stories. The ground plans reflect more or less the character of the site they occupy, and we would be as much surprised to find plans of their character in the open country as we are to see plans of class I within the canyon. Unlike the ground plans of class I, those of this group were laid out with direct reference to the cliff behind them, and which formed, as it were, a part of them.

In point of size, long period of occupancy, and position these villages were the most important in the canyon. The ruins often cover considerable areas and almost invariably show the remains of one or more circular kivas. Sometimes they are located directly upon the bottom land, more often they occupy low swells next the cliff, rising perhaps 10 feet above the general level and affording a fine view over it. Sometimes they are found in alcoves at the base of the cliff, but they always rest on the bottom land which extends into them; these merge insensibly into the next class—village ruins on defensible sites—and the distinction between them is partly an arbitrary one, as is also that between the last mentioned and the cliff ruins proper.

Figure 1 is a ground plan of a small ruin located in Del Muerto, on the bottom lands near its mouth. No standing walls now remain,

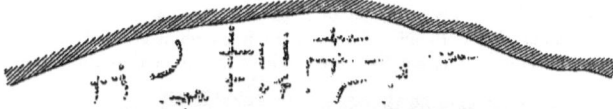

FIG. 1—Ground plan of an old ruin in Canyon del Muerto.

but there is no doubt that the village at one time covered much more ground than that shown on the plan. There are now remains of sixteen rooms on the ground, in addition to two kivas. There is a shallow alcove in the cliff at the ground level, and the overhanging cliff gave the village some protection overhead. Plate XLV shows another example in Del Muerto, the largest in that canyon. The walls are still standing to a height of three stories in one place, and the masonry is of high class. The back cliff has not entered into the plan here to the same extent that it generally does. Figure 2, a ground plan, exhibits only that portion of the area of the ruin on which walls are still standing. It shows about 20 rooms on the ground, exclusive of three or perhaps four kivas. The rooms are small as a rule, rectangular, and arranged with a more than ordinary degree of regularity. One room still carries its roof intact, as shown on the plan. In the center of the ruin are the remains of a very large kiva, over 36 feet in diameter. It is now so much broken down that but little can be inferred as to its former condition, except that there was probably no interior bench, as no remains of such a structure can now be distinguished. The size of this kiva is exceptional, and it is very probable that it was never roofed. The structures within the kiva, shown on the ground plan, are Navaho burial cists. West of the large kiva there were two others, less than 20 feet in diameter. One of these was circular; the other was irregular in shape, perhaps more nearly approaching an oval form.

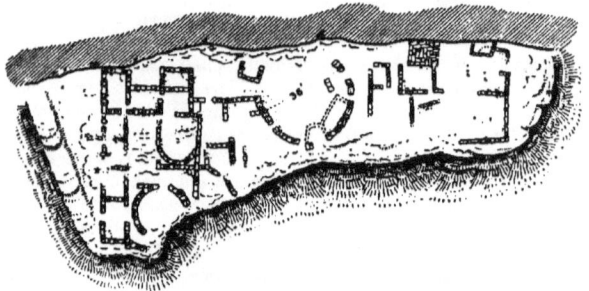

Fig. 2—Ground plan of a ruin on bottom land in Canyon del Muerto.

At no fewer than five places within the ruin there are comparatively recent Navaho burials.

Figure 3 is a ground plan of a small and very compact village, situated on the south side of the canyon at the point marked 28 on the detailed map. It is located on a slightly raised part of the bottom,

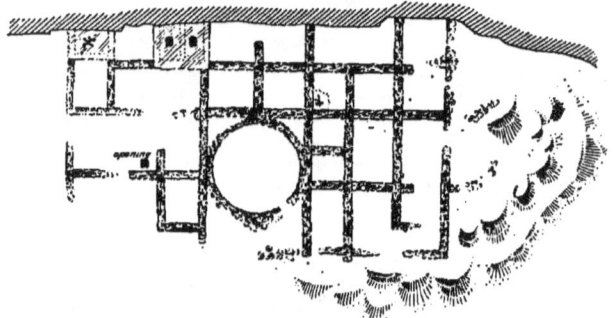

Fig. 3—Ground plan of a small ruin in Canyon de Chelly.

commanding an outlook over a large area now under cultivation by the Navaho. The wall lines are remarkably, although not perfectly, regular, and show at least 25 rooms; there were probably others to the northward and eastward. The rooms are now almost filled with débris, but two of them are still intact, being kept in order by the Navaho

GENERAL VIEW OF RUIN ON BOTTOM LAND, CANYON DEL MUERTO

and used for the storage of corn. The roofs of both these rooms are now on the ground level. The covered room nearest the cliff, shown on the plan, has been divided into two small compartments by a wall through the middle; access to each of these is obtained by a framed trapdoor in the roof about a foot square. This dividing wall is probably of Navaho origin, as the separate rooms formed by it are too small for habitation and the masonry is very rough. A short distance to the north along the cliff there is a Navaho house, roughly rectangular in plan, which was constructed of stone obtained from this site. The masonry of the ruin presents a very good face, not due to chinking, however, which was but slightly practiced, but to the careful selection of material. Some of the stones show surface pecking.

About 300 feet above or southeast of this ruin there are the remains of two small rooms which were placed against the cliff. They are of the same general character as those described, and doubtless formed part of the same settlement. Between the two occurs a curious feature. A large slab of rock, 280 feet long and not more than 12 feet thick at any point, has split off from the cliff and dropped down to the ground, where it remains on edge. This slab is triangular in elevation and about 50 feet high at the apex. Between it and the cliff, in the upper

Fig. 4—Granary in the rocks, connected with a ruin.

part, there is a space from 2 to 2½ feet wide. This is easily accessible from the north, on the edge of the slab, and can be reached from the southern end, but with much difficulty. Figure 4 shows this feature and its relation to the ruin. There is no doubt that this was a granary or huge storage bin, and probably the two rooms on the south were placed there to guard that end; the northern end, of more easy access, being protected by the village itself. It was well adapted to this purpose—a fact that the Navaho have not been slow to appreciate. They have constructed small bins near the northern end, shown on the plan, and beyond this timbers have been wedged in so as to furnish a means of closing the cleft. In the cleft itself cross walls have been constructed, dividing it into several compartments. The interior forms a convenient dry, airy space, and at the time it was visited the floor was covered with a litter of cornhusks.

Almost directly opposite this ruin, on the other side of the canyon, are the remains of a village that might properly be called a cave village. At this point a large rock stands out from the cliff and in it there is a cavity shaped almost like a quarter sphere. Its greatest diameter is 45 feet and its height about 20 feet. The bottom land here is 10 or 12 feet above the stream bed and slopes up gradually toward

16 ETH——7

the cliff, forming the bottom of the cave, which is perhaps 18 or 20 feet above the stream and some distance from it. The cave commands an extensive outlook over the cultivable lands below it and those extending up a branch canyon a little above.

The whole bottom of the cave is covered by remains of rooms, shown in plan in figure 5. The population could not have been greater than 10 or 12 persons, yet the remains of two kivas are clearly shown. Both were in the front of the cave, adjoining but not connected with each other, and were about 12 feet in diameter. Both had interior benches, extending in one perhaps completely around, in the other only partly around. The rooms are very irregular in shape and in size, ranging from 8 by 10 feet to 3 by 4 feet, but the latter could be used only for storage. The masonry is not of fine grade, although good; but not much detail can be made out, as the place has been used as a

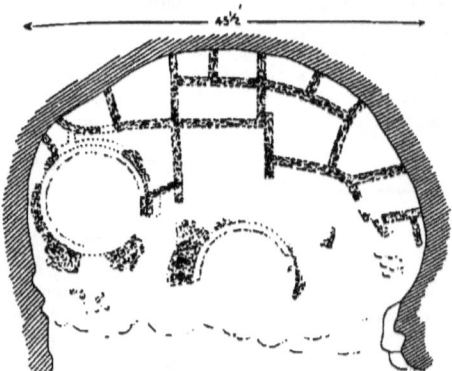

Fig. 5—Ground plan of a ruin in a cave.

sheepfold by the Navaho and the ground surface has been filled up and smoothed over.

The largest ruin in the canyons is that shown in plan in figure 6. It is situated in Del Muerto, on the canyon bottom at the base of a cliff, and is known to the Navaho as Pakashi-izini (the blue cow). The name was derived probably from a pictograph of a cow done in blue paint on the canyon wall back of the ruin. Traces of walls extend over a narrow belt against the cliffs about 400 feet long and not over 40 feet wide, and over this area many walls are still standing. Scattered over the site are a number of large bowlders. No attempt to remove these was made, but walls were carried over and under them, and in some cases the direction of a wall was modified to correspond with a face of a bowlder.

The settlement may have consisted of two separate portions, divided by a row or cluster of large bowlders. The group shown on the right

of the plan was very compactly built, in
one place being four rooms deep, but no
traces of a kiva can be seen in it, nor does
there appear to be any place where a kiva
could be built within the house area or
immediately adjacent to it. At present
14 or 15 rooms may be traced on the
ground and the whole structure may
have comprised 30 rooms. The wall lines
are not regular. In the western end of
the structure there is a narrow passageway into a large room in the center.
Such passageways, while often seen in
the valley pueblos, are rare in these canyons. The three rooms to the south of
the passageway appear to have been
added after the rest of the structure was
completed, and diminished in size regularly by a series of steps or insets in the
northern or passage wall.

The other portion of the ruin shows the
remains of about 40 rooms on the ground,
in addition to three kivas; there may have
been 60 rooms in this part of the settlement, or 85 or 90 rooms altogether. The
population could not have been over 55
or 60 persons, or about 12 families. In
other words, it appears that, owing to the
peculiarities of conditions under which
they lived, and of the ground plan which
resulted, the largest settlement of this
class in the canyons, extending over 400
feet in one direction, provided homes for
a very limited number of people. As it is
probable that each family had one or more
outlooks, occupied in connection with their
horticultural operations, it will readily be
seen that only a small number of inhabitants might leave a large number of house
remains, and that it is not necessary to
assume either a large population or a long
period of occupancy.

The kivas are clustered in the lower
end of the settlement, and all appear to
have been inclosed within walls or other
buildings. Two of them are fairly well
preserved; of the third only a fragment

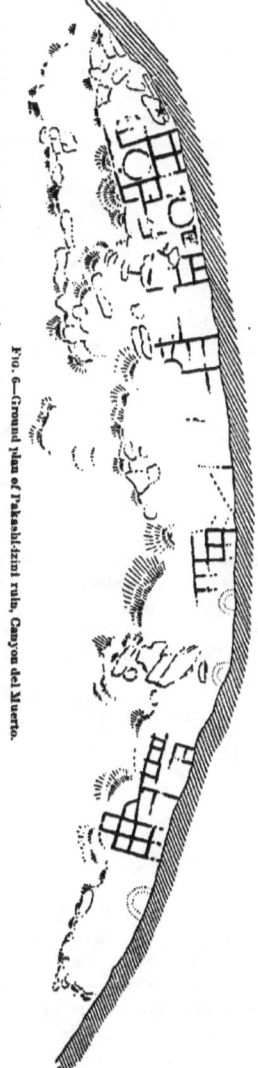

FIG. 6—Ground plan of Pakashi-izini ruin, Canyon del Muerto.

remains. The inclosure of the kivas is a suggestive feature, which will be discussed later, as will also the square shaft shown on the plan as attached to the principal kiva.

It will be noticed that in several places where bowlders occur within the limits of the settlement they have been incorporated into the walls and form part of them. In two places they have altered the direction of walls and produced irregularities in the plan. Elsewhere the face

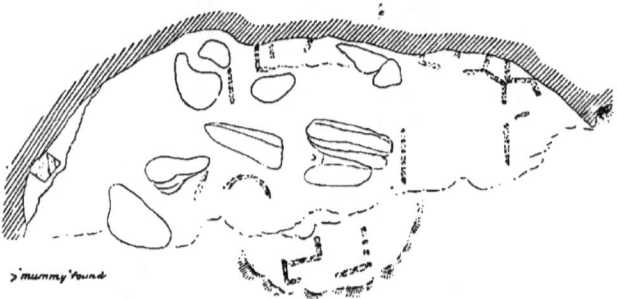

FIG. 7—Ground plan of a ruin in Canyon del Muerto.

of a rock has been prolonged by a wall carried out to continue it, as in the front wall of the principal kiva apartment. This apartment appears to have been entered from the west through a passageway. This is an anomalous feature and suggests modernness.

Figure 7 is a ground plan of another ruin in Del Muerto. There is a slight cove or bay in the cliff at the point where the ruin occurs, and the ground, which is on the level of the bottom lands, is strewn

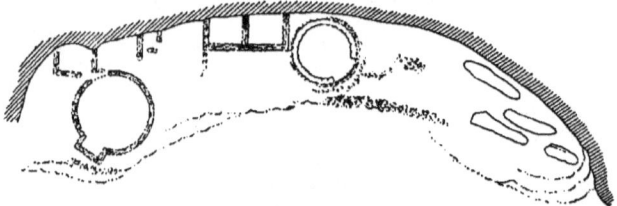

FIG. 8—Ground plan of a ruin in Tseonitsosi canyon.

with large bowlders, as in the example last described. But few remains of walls are now observable, and there are traces of only one kiva. This was situated near the outer edge of the settlement. The wall lines are irregular and the disposition and size of the bowlders are such that it is improbable that this site was ever occupied by a large cluster of rooms. On the left of the plan will be seen a small room or storage cist still intact. At the point marked > in the center of the site a burial cist was found and excavated in 1884 by Mr Thomas V. Keam. It contained the remains of a child, almost perfectly desiccated. It is said that when the remains were first removed the color of the iris could be distinguished. The specimen was subsequently deposited in the National Museum.

A ruin which occurs in Tse-ou-i-tso-si canyon, near the mouth of De Chelly, is shown in plan in figure 8. There were two kivas, one of which was benched. The number of rooms connected with them is remarkably small—there could not have been more than six, if there were that many—and the character of the site is such as to preclude

Fig. 9—Ground plan of a much obliterated ruin.

the possibility of other rooms in the immediate vicinity. Some of the walls are still standing, and exhibit a fair degree of skill in masonry.

A type of which there are many examples is shown in plan in figure 9. These ruins occur on the flat, next the cliff, which is seldom bayed and overhangs but slightly. They are usually so much obliterated that only careful scrutiny reveals the presence of wall lines, and walls standing to a height of 6 inches above the ground are rare. In the example illustrated no traces of a kiva can be found, but the almost complete destruction of the walls might account for this. There is every reason to suppose that these ruins are of the same class as those

Fig. 10—Ground plan of a ruin in Canyon de Chelly.

described above, the remains of home villages located without reference to defense, and no reason to suppose otherwise. They are probably instances where, owing to exposed situation, early abandonment, and possibly also proximity to later establishments, destruction has proceeded at a greater rate than in other examples.

Ruins of the class under discussion were not confined to any part of the canyons, but were located wherever the conditions were favorable. An example which occurs in the lower part of the canyon, at the point marked 3 on the map, is shown in plan in figure 10. It occurs at the back of a deep cove in a little branch canyon, and was at one time quite an extensive village. It was located on a slight slope or raised place next the cliffs and overhung by them. A stone dropped from the top of the cliffs would fall 45 or 50 feet out from their base. There are remains of three kivas. The central one, which was 12 feet in diameter, still shows nearly all its periphery, and the wall is in one place 3 feet high. The western kiva is now almost obliterated, but it can still be made out, and shows a diameter of 15 feet. It is 50 feet west of the central kiva and on a level about 8 feet below it, being only about 3 feet above the bottom land. East of the central kiva, and between it and a large bowlder, there was another, of which only a part now remains.

North of the central kiva, and extending nearly to the cliff behind, there are remains of rooms. One corner is still standing to a height of 3 to 4 feet. The western wall was smoothly plastered outside and was pierced by a narrow notched doorway. The northern wall has an opening still intact, shown in plate LVIII; it is 2 feet high and 14 inches wide, with a lintel composed of six small sticks about an inch in diameter, laid side by side. The sticks are surmounted by a flat stone, very roughly shaped and separated from them by an inch of mud plaster or mortar. The masonry is exceptionally well executed, that of the northern wall being composed of large stones carefully chinked and rubbed down. The chinking appears to have been carried through in bands, producing a decorative effect, resembling some of the masonry of the Chaco ruins. The western wall is composed of larger stones laid up more roughly with less chinking, and appears to have been a later addition. On the back wall of the cave are marks of walls showing a number of additional rooms, and there is no doubt that at one time there was quite an extensive settlement here.

Around the corner from the last example, as it were (at the point marked 4 on the map), and at the mouth of a little canyon that opens out from the head of the cove, the ruin shown in plate XLVI occurs. The village was located on the canyon bottom, in a shallow cove hardly 25 feet deep, but the view over the bottom is almost closed by a large sand dune, bare on top and but scantily covered on the sides with grass and weeds. Were it not for this dune, the site of the ruin would command one of the best areas of cultivable land in the canyon, but apparently an extensive outlook was not a desideratum. The slight elevation of the site above the level of the bottom lands is shown in the illustration.

The village was not a large one, having been occupied probably by only two families, yet there are traces of two kivas. That on the west is so far obliterated that its outline can be made out only with difficulty. That on the east still shows a part of its wall to a height of about a foot. The plan, figure 11, shows the general arrangement. Some of the walls are still standing to a height of 2 or 3 feet, and at the eastern end of the ruin there is a room with walls 6 feet high. More than the usual amount of mud mortar was used in the construction of

VILLAGE RUIN IN CANYON DE CHELLY

the walls of this room, and the interstices were filled with this, chinking with small stones being but slightly practiced. The masonry of the other walls is rougher, with even less chinking, and some of them show later additions which did not follow the main lines. The eastern room had two openings and the tops of the walls are apparently finished, for there are no marks of roof timbers. The room may have been roofless, but the same effect might have been produced by recent Navaho repairs and alterations. In the exterior wall, at the southeastern corner, there

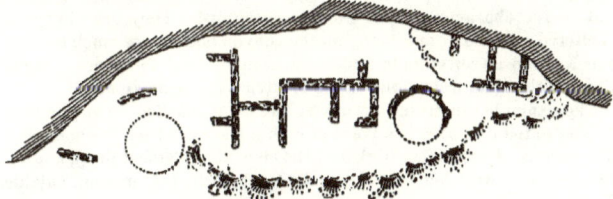

Fig. 11—Ground plan of a village ruin.

is a series of hand-holes, as though access to the interior were sometimes had in this way, but the hand-holes are later than the wall. On the back wall of the cove there are a number of pictographs.

Just above the mouth of Del Muerto and on the opposite side of the main canyon, at the point marked 17 on the map, there was a village on the canyon bottom. It overlooked a fine stretch of cultivable land on both sides of the canyon. There is a large isolated mass of rock here, nearly as high as the cliffs on either side, and connected with

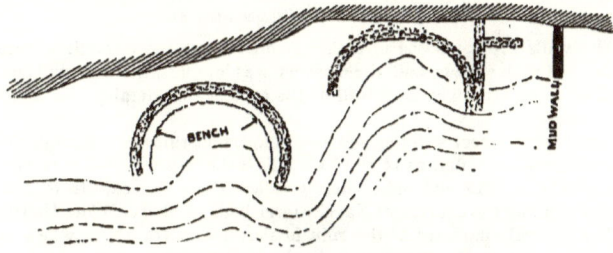

Fig. 12—Ground plan of kivas in Canyon de Chelly.

those back of it by a slope of talus and débris, partly bare rock, partly covered with sand dunes. At the point where the ruin occurs the rock is bare and about 40 feet high, partly overhanging the site. The remains, shown in plan in figure 12, occupy the summit of a hill about 10 feet high, composed principally of débris of walls. Only a few faint traces now remain, but two kivas are still clearly distinguishable. The one on the south had an interior bench, which apparently extended around it. The other shows walls 2 feet high, and has been plastered with a number of successive coats. The small wall on the extreme right of the plan is composed of almost pure mud.

There are a number of ruins in the canyons of the type shown in figure 13. They are generally located directly on the bottom, and seldom as much as 5 feet above it, within coves or under overhanging cliffs; they are always of small area, and generally so far obliterated that no walls or wall remains are now visible. The obliteration is due not so much to antiquity, which may or may not have been a cause, but to the character of the site they occupied. They are always in sheltered situations, and being on the canyon bottom are much used by the Navaho as sheepfolds and have been so used for years. Sometimes, although rarely, faint traces of kivas can be made out.

The example illustrated occurs at the point marked 43 on the map. It is situated in a cove in a point of rock jutting out from the main cliff. The rock is about 60 feet high and the cove about 30 feet deep, and the remains are but a few feet above the level of the bottom land outside.

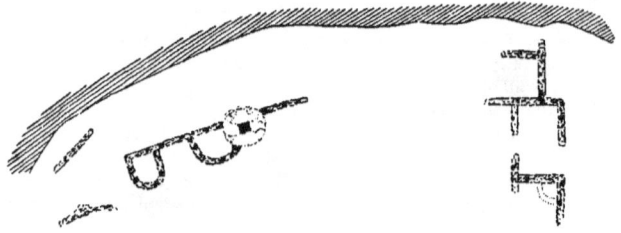

Fig. 13.—Ground plan of a small ruin on bottom land.

The walls are composed of rather small stones; the interstices were chinked with spawls, and the masonry was laid up with an abundance of mud mortar. The back wall of the cove is considerably blackened by smoke.

One of the most striking and most important ruins in the canyon is shown in plan in figures 14 and 15. This is the ruin seen by Lieutenant Simpson in 1849 and subsequently called Casa Blanca. It is also known under the equivalent Navaho term, Kini-na e-kai or White House. The general character of the ruin is shown in plate XLVII, which is from a photograph. At first sight this ruin appears not to belong to this class, or rather to belong both to this class and the succeeding one composed of villages located with reference to defense; but, as will appear later, it has nothing in common with the latter.

In its present condition the ruin consists of two distinct parts—a lower part, comprising a large cluster of rooms on the bottom land against the vertical cliff, and an upper part which was much smaller and occupied a cave directly over the lower portion and was separated

BUREAU OF AMERICAN ETHNOLOGY

CASA BLANCA RUIN, CANYON DE CHELLY

from it only by some 35 feet
of vertical cliff. There is evidence, however, that some of
the houses in the lower settlement were four stories high
against the cliff, and in fact
that the structures were
practically continuous; but
for convenience of description we may regard the ruin
as composed of two.

The lower ruin covers an
area of about 150 by 50 feet,
raised but a few feet above
the bottom land, probably
by its own débris. Within
this area there are remains
of 45 rooms on the ground,
in addition to a circular
kiva. On the east side there
are walls still standing to a
height of 12 and 14 feet. It
is probable that the lower
ruin comprised about 60
rooms, which, with a liberal
allowance for the rooms in
the cave, would make a total
of 80. This would furnish
accommodations for a maximum of 10 or 12 families or
a total population of 50 or
60 persons. It is probable,
however, that this estimate
is excessive and that the
total population at any one
time did not exceed 30 or 40
persons.

The ground plans shown
are the result of a very careful survey, plotted on the
ground on a large scale (10
feet to 1 inch—1:120), and
the irregularities shown were
carefully noted and put down
at the time. These irregularities, which are commonly
ignored in the preparation

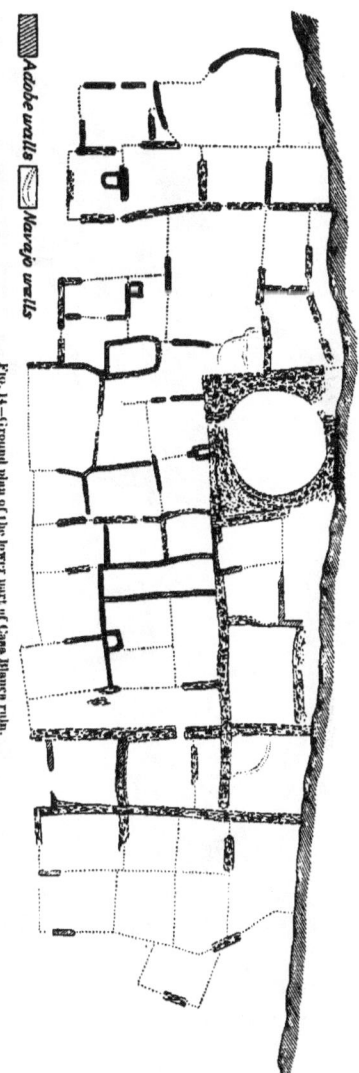

Adobe walls   Navajo walls

FIG. 14—Ground plans of the lower part of Casa Blanca ruin.

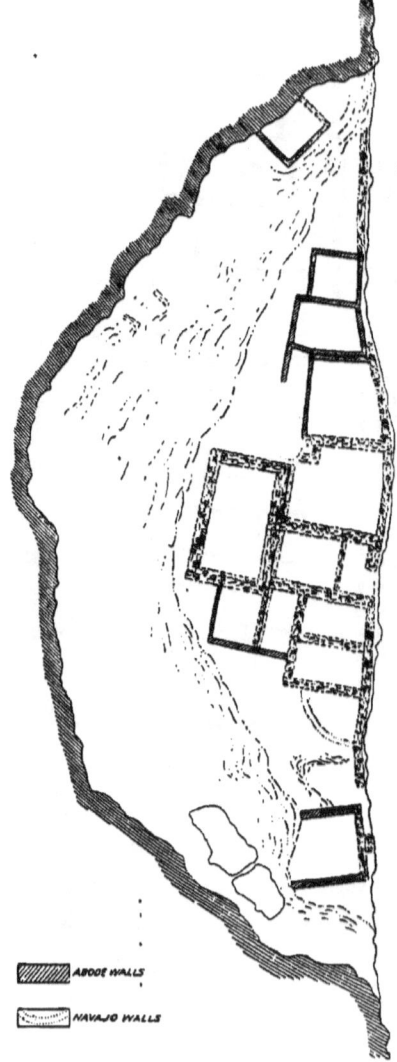

FIG. 15—Ground plan of the upper part of Casa Blanca ruin.

ABODE WALLS

NAVAJO WALLS

of plans of ruins, are of the highest importance. From them the sequence of construction can often be determined.

The walls of the lower ruin are somewhat obscured by loose débris, of which a large amount is lying about. Roof débris is especially abundant; it consists of small twigs and lumps of clay, with ends of beams projecting here and there. The principal walls occur in the eastern part, where some of them are 2 feet thick and still standing to a height of 10 and 12 and in one place of 14 feet. An inspection of the plan will show that, as is invariably the case where a wall rises to a height of more than one story, the lower part is massive and the upper wall sets back 5 or 6 inches, reducing its thickness by that amount. All the heavy walls occur either about the kiva or east of it. Apparently these walls were built first especially heavy and massive, and afterward, when upper stories were added, it was not found necessary to carry them up the full thickness. It will be noticed that the wall extending eastward from the corner of

the kiva, and which is from a foot to 6 feet high at the present time,
extends through the heavy wall which crosses it 33 feet to the east, and
is continuous to its termination about 50 feet east, against another
heavy wall. The last-mentioned wall is also continuous from the cliff
out to the front of the ruin, a distance of about 46 feet.

The heavy walls of the lower ruin are immediately under the upper
cave. Back of them the cliff presents an almost smooth face of rock,
35 feet high and slightly overhanging. On this rock face there are
marks which show that formerly there were upper stories, the rooms of
which are outlined upon it. The rock surface was coated in places with
a thin wash of clay, doubtless to correspond with the other walls of the
rooms, but this coating was necessarily omitted where the partition
walls and roofs and floors abutted on the rock. This is shown in plate
XLVII. Although the marks are now so faint as to be easily overlooked, at a certain hour in the day, when the light falls obliquely on
the rock, they can be clearly made out. At a point about 50 feet east
of the kiva the structure was three stories higher than it is now. The
roof of the upper story was within 4 feet of the floor of the cave, and
under the gap or gateway in front of the main room above. West of this
point there are the marks of but two stories additional. Farther west
the structure rose again, but not to the height attained on the east.

The kiva was placed directly against the cliff. This is an unusual
arrangement; but it will be noticed that the walls in front of it are of
a different character from those on the east, and it is probable that
when the kiva was built it opened to the air. The kiva is also anomalous in its construction. It presents the usual features of the inner
circular chamber and an inclosing rectangular wall, but in this case
the intermediate space was filled in solidly, and perhaps was so constructed. The kiva is still 6 feet deep inside, which must be nearly its
maximum depth, and the roof was probably placed at a level not more
than a foot or two above the present top. Whether the village was
placed on a slight raise, or on the flat, level with the bottom land about
it, and subsequently filled up with the débris of masonry, etc, can not
be determined without excavation; but the top of the kiva is now 16
feet above the general level of the bottom land, and its bottom 10 feet
above that level. It is possible that the kiva was much deeper than now
appears, as no sign of the usual interior bench can be seen above the
present ground surface, nor can any connection with the chimney-like
structure to the south of it be determined, yet such connection must
have existed. Probably not only this kiva but the whole ruin would
well repay excavation.

The interior of the kiva was not exactly circular, being a little elongated northeast and southwest. The inclosing wall on the east is still
standing in one place to a height of 5 feet above the top of the kiva
structure, and about a foot above that level is marked by a setback,
which reduces its thickness. Apparently the upper part was added at

a date some time subsequent to the completion of the kiva structure, as the wall on the south, now some 3 feet above the level mentioned, does not conform to the lower exterior wall on which it was placed. On the western side there is another fragment of the upper inclosing wall. Both this wall and the one on the south are less than 15 inches in thickness.

West of the kiva there are remains of other stone walls which differ in character from those on the east. They are now usually less than 3 feet high; they were 12 to 15 inches thick, and the lines are very irregular. South of the kiva, in the center of the ruin, there are other stone walls even thinner and more irregularly placed than those on the west, but most of the walls here are of adobe. As the use of adobe blocks is not an aboriginal feature, the occurrence of these walls is a matter of much interest, especially as they are so intimately associated with the stonework that it is not always an easy matter to separate them.

The occurrence and distribution of adobe walls is shown on the ground plan. They are not found as subordinate walls, dividing larger rooms, except perhaps in one instance; but apparently this method of construction was employed when it was desired to add new rooms to those already constructed. No room with walls constructed wholly of adobe can be made out, but walls of this character closing one side of a room are common, and rooms with two or even three sides of adobe are not uncommon. There are some instances in which part of a wall is stone and part adobe, and also instances in which the lower wall, complete in itself, is of stone, while the upper part, evidently a later addition, is of adobe; such, for example, is the cross wall in the eastern tier, about 30 feet from the cliff.

The mere occurrence of adobe here is evidence of the occupancy of this site at a period subsequent to the sixteenth century—we might almost say subsequent to the middle of the seventeenth; but its occurrence in this way and in such intimate association with the stone walls indicates that the occupancy was continuous from a time prior to the introduction of adobe construction to a period some time subsequent to it. This hypothesis is supported by other evidence, which will appear later. Attention may here be directed to the fact that there are four chimney-like structures in the lower ruin, all of adobe, and all, except the one which pertains to the kiva, attached to adobe walls.

On the western margin of the ruin, and nowhere else within it, there are traces of another kind of construction which was not found elsewhere within the canyon. This method is known to the Mexicans as "jacal," and much used by them. It consists of a row of sticks or thin poles set vertically in the ground and heavily plastered with mud. At present not one of these walls remains to a height of 6 inches above the ground, but the lines of poles broken off at the ground level are still visible. The ground at this point is but 3 or 4 feet above the general level of the bottom. The ground plan shows the occurrence of these wall remains on the western edge of the site. They are all outside of but attached to what was formerly the exterior wall on that side.

There are remains of four Navaho burial cists in the lower ruin, at the points shown on the ground plan. These are constructed of stones and mud roughly put together in the ordinary manner, forming thin, rounded walls; but these can not be confounded with the other methods of construction described. Three of the cists have long been in ruins and broken down; the one on the east is but a few years old.

Access to the upper ruin can now be had only with much difficulty. In the western end of the cave there is a single room placed on the cliff edge, and between this and the end of a wall to the right a small stick has been embedded in the masonry at a height of about 2 feet from the rock. The cliff here is vertical and affords no footing, but by throwing a rope over the stick a man can ascend hand over hand. During the period when the houses were occupied, access was had in another and much easier way, through a doorway or passageway nearly in the center of the ruin and directly over the point where the lower village was four stories high. The roof of the lower structure was less than 4 feet below the floor of the cave; yet there is no doubt that a doorway or passageway existed also at the western end of the cave, as the western end of the wall on the right of the stick is neatly finished and apparently complete.

The principal room in the upper ruin is situated nearly in the center of the cave, and is the one that has given the whole ruin its name. The walls are 2 feet thick, constructed of stone, 12 feet high in front and 7 feet high on the sides and inside. The exterior was finished with a coat of whitewash, with a decorative band in yellow; hence the name of Casa Blanca or White House. West of the principal room there is a smaller one, which appears to be a later addition. The walls of this room are only 7 inches thick, of adobe on the sides and back and of small stones in front. The top of the wall is about 2 feet below the top of the wall on the east. The coat of whitewash and the yellow decorative band are continuous over both rooms, but the white coat was also applied to the exterior western wall of the main room. In the main room there is a series of small sticks, about half an inch in diameter, projecting 8 inches from the wall and on a line 3 or 4 inches under where the roof was.

The small room in the eastern end of the cave was located on a kind of bench or upper level, and was constructed partly of stone and partly of adobe. The stone part is the upper portion of the eastern half. On the west there is a small opening or window, with an appliance for closing it. It is probable that this room was used only for storage. In the western end of the cave there is another single room, which is clearly shown in plate XLVII. The front wall is 11 feet high outside and 5 feet high inside. The lower portion is stone, the upper part and sides are adobe, and the side walls rest on nearly 2 feet of straw, ashes, etc. The buttress shown in the illustration is of stone and the front wall that it supports is slightly battened. A close inspection of the illustration will show that this wall rests partly on horizontal timber work, a feature which is repeated in several walls in the main cluster of the ruins.

The use of timber laid horizontally under a wall is not uncommon, and as it will be discussed at greater length in another place, it may be dismissed here with the statement that as a rule it failed to accomplish the purpose intended. But the use of the buttress is an anomalous feature which it is difficult to believe was of aboriginal conception. Its occurrence in this ruin together with so many other unaboriginal features is suggestive.

The walls of the principal room and of the rooms immediately in front of it are constructed of stone; all the other walls in the upper ruin are of adobe or have adobe in them. The two rooms on the east and two walls of the room adjoining on the west are wholly of adobe, about 7 inches thick and now 3 and 4 feet high. In the southeast corner of the second room from the east there is an opening through the front wall which may have been a drain. It is on the floor level, round, 5 inches in diameter, and smoothly plastered. In the fourth room from the east there is a similar hole. Both of these discharge on the edge of the cliff, and it is difficult to imagine their purpose unless they were expedients for draining the rooms; but this would imply that the rooms were not roofed. Although the cliff above is probably 500 feet high, and overhangs to the degree that a rock pushed over its edge falls 15 feet or more outside of the outermost wall remains, and over 70 feet from the foot of the cliff, still a driving storm of rain or snow would leave considerable quantities of water in the front rooms if they were not roofed, and some means would have to be provided to carry it off.

In the same room, the fourth from the east, there are the remains of a chimney-like structure, the only one in the upper ruin. It is in the northeast corner, at a point where the wall has fallen and been replaced by a Navaho burial cist also fallen in ruin, and was constructed of stone. There is no doubt that it was added some time after the walls were built, as it has cracked off from the wall on the east, which shows at that point its original finish. In the eastern wall of this room there is a well-finished opening, and at the corresponding point in the wall of the room on the right, the third wall from the east, there is another. The latter wall is of adobe, or rather there are two adobe walls built side by side; one, the eastern, considerably thinner than the other. The opening extends through both walls; it was neatly finished and was closed by a thin slab of stone plastered in with mud. It has the appliance for closing mentioned above and described later (page 165). Most of the openings in the walls appear to have been closed up at the time the houses were abandoned.

The front wall of the main room is 12 feet high in front and was stepped back 6 inches at half its height from the ground. The step-back is continued through the front wall of the small room on the west. Near the center of the main room there is a well-finished door-way, directly over the point where a cross wall in front of it comes in. This opening was originally a double-notched or T-shape doorway, but at a later period was filled up so as to leave only a rectangular orifice. The principal entrance to the upper ruin was in front of this opening and a little to the left of it. It will be noticed from an inspection of the plan that the room into which this entrance opened was divided at a point about 4 feet back from the cliff edge by a stone wall not more than half the thickness of the walls on either side of it. This cross wall is still 6 feet high on the side nearest the cliff, but there is no evidence of a doorway or opening through it. The back rooms must have been reached by a ladder in front, thence over the roof of the room. The cliff entrance was a narrow doorway left in the front wall. The ends of the walls on either side were smoothly finished, as in the western doorway.

There are many lumps of clay scattered about on the ground, some showing impressions of small sticks. Apparently they are the débris of roofs. There are also some fragments of pottery, principally corru-gated ware. The adobe walls in the upper ruin rest generally on rock, sometimes on ashes and loose débris; in the lower ruin they rest usu-ally on stone foundations. The occurrence in this ruin of many fea-tures that are not aboriginal suggests that it was one of the last to be abandoned in the canyon, but there are certain features which make it seem probable that the upper portion continued to be inhabited for some time after the lower portion. The contrivance for closing open-ings is identical with examples found in the Mesa Verde region, and it is probable that an intimate connection between the two existed.

III—HOME VILLAGES LOCATED FOR DEFENSE

The distinction between home villages located on bottom lands abso-lutely without reference to the defensive value of the site, and other villages located on defensive sites, is to some extent an arbitrary one. The former, which are always located at the base of or under an over-hanging cliff, sometimes occupy slightly raised ground which overlooks the adjacent land, and the latter are sometimes so slightly raised above the bottoms they overlook as hardly to come within the classification. Moreover, ruins in their present condition sometimes belong to both classes, as in the example last described. Yet a general distinction may be drawn between the classes, in that the former are generally located directly upon the bottom land and invariably without thought or regard to the defensive value of the site, while in the latter the effect of this requirement is always apparent.

The class of ruins which has been designated as the remains of vil-lages located for defense comprises all the most striking remains in the canyon, many of which may properly be termed cliff ruins. The characteristics of the class are: A site more or less difficult of access—generally an elaborate ground plan, although sometimes they consist of only a few rooms—and the invariable presence of the kiva or estufa, here always circular in form. The largest ruin of this class occurs in Del Muerto, and is known as Mummy Cave ruin. It is called by the Navaho Tse-i-ya-kin. It is situated in the upper part of the canyon, near the junction of a small branch, and has an extensive outlook.

At a height of about 80 feet above the top of a gentle slope of earth and loose rock, and perhaps 300 feet above the stream bed, there are two coves in the rock, connected by a narrow bench. The western cove is about 100 feet across and its back is perhaps 75 feet from the front wall of the cliff. The eastern cove is over 200 feet across and perhaps 100 feet deep, while the connecting ledge is about 110 feet long. Ruins occur on the central ledge and on similar ledges in the back parts of both coves.

The western or smaller cove is accessible only from the ledge, which in turn can be approached only from the eastern cove. The smaller cove had a row of little rooms across the back and there are traces of walls on the slope in front of these. Fourteen rooms can now be made out on the ground; altogether there may have been 20 rooms in this portion. Practically all the available space on the ledge was occupied by rooms, and 10, all of considerable size, can now be traced. The total number in this portion was 14 or 15. The eastern cove contained the largest part of the settlement. The back part is occupied by a ledge about 50 feet wide entirely covered by remains of walls. Some 44 rooms can now be made out on the ground, in addition to 3 or perhaps 4 circular kivas, and the whole number of rooms may have been 55. Assuming, then, that the various portions of the ruin were inhabited at the same time, we would have a total of 90 rooms; but, as many of them could be used only for storage, the population could not have been more than 60 persons.

The rooms in the western cove are fairly uniform in size and were probably habitations, for they are all too large to be classed as storage rooms. There was no kiva in this portion, however, nor any unoccupied place where a kiva might have been placed. It seems clear, therefore, that this portion was either an appendage of the other or was occupied at a later period; in either case it was constructed at a date subsequent to the remains in the eastern cove.

The intermediate ledge, which is about 110 feet long and about 30 feet wide, was practically all occupied by a row of seven rooms, some of them of more than one story. These rooms are exceptionally large—larger than any group of rooms in the canyon or in this part of the country. The outside or front wall is more than 20 feet from the cliff back of it, and the rooms are from 10 to 15 feet wide. Figure 16, which is a ground plan of the ruin, shows the exceptional size of

MUMMY CAVE, CENTRAL AND EASTERN PART

these rooms. All of them were at least two stories high; some were three. The walls in this portion are generally 2 feet or more thick and exceptionally well constructed. Its eastern end is still standing to a height of three stories, and carries a roof intact, giving a tower-like effect to that portion. Originally this portion rose but one story above the other rooms. Throughout nearly all its length the front wall shows part of the upper story, which is also marked on the cliff wall by a thin wash of clay, in the same manner as in the Casa Blanca ruin. The two rooms west of the tower were surmounted by a single large room. The cliff wall is coated with a thin wash of yellowish clay, and no mark of a cross wall or partition can be seen upon it. There are no openings between the three eastern rooms on the ground floor. The first room to the west of the tower has a square chimney-like shaft, and a niche or alcove connected with it. The second room also has a niche and a rounded shaft. The third room has neither niche nor shaft.

The front wall was exceptionally heavy, but the upper portion has fallen inward, forming a heavy mass of débris against it. The east and south sides of the tower, for about 5 feet of its height, are decorated by inlaying small stones 1 to 2 inches long and half an inch thick. The same decoration occurs at intervals down the front wall, but irregularly. This feature is not chinking, such as has been described, and has no constructive value, but is purely decorative. Back of the rooms west of the tower there are some old pictographs on

16 ETH——8

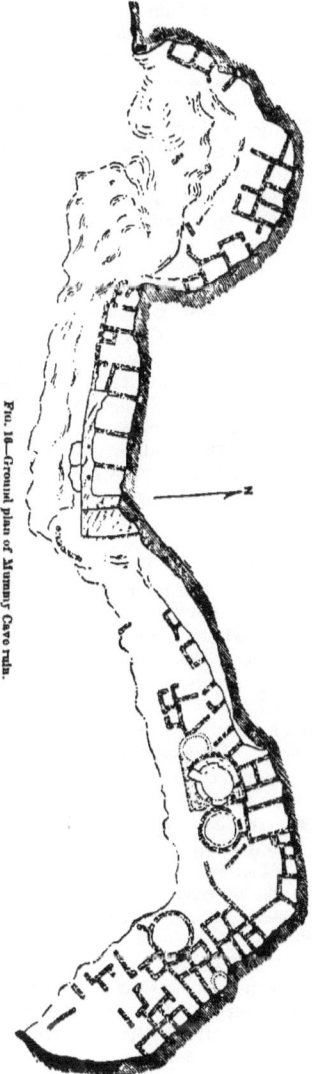

Fig. 16—Ground plan of Mummy Cave ruin.

the cliff wall at the place where the roof abutted on it. Here the wash of clay before mentioned was necessarily omitted. In the first room there is a pictograph of a man, in the second a semicircle, both done in light-green paint.

The lower part of the outer corner of the tower has fallen out. At this point there was a small doorway or opening, which was the only entrance on the south or east. The corner which has fallen was apparently supported by three or four sticks laid horizontally on the rock at an angle of 45 degrees with either wall. The giving way of the timber support apparently caused the fall of the corner, but why a structure otherwise so substantial should be placed on such frail support, when a filling of masonry was both easy and practicable, is not clear.

The doorway mentioned is the only opening into the ground-floor room in the tower. Connection with the rooms on the west was through a large doorway in the western wall of the second story, and in the story above there was a similar opening. These are shown in plate XLVIII, which is a general view of the central portion of the eastern cove.

The lintels of the openings in the central part are formed of round sticks, about 3 inches in diameter, matched, and bound together with withes. These withes may be seen in places where the mud plaster has fallen away. The stick lintels occur only in the central portion; the windows and doorways of the other portions of the ruin, some fine examples of which remain, are always finished with stone lintels and sometimes with stone jambs.

A little east of the center of the front wall there is a large rock, or rather a pile of large rocks, near the outer edge of the ledge. This is shown in the illustration. Instead of removing this obstruction the wall was built under and over it. Near the western end of the front wall there is a large doorway or opening. Access to the western cove was along the narrow edge of the ledge under the front wall, thence through this doorway. The doorway gave entrance to a very narrow space, less than 4 feet square, surrounded by a heavy wall with a doorway through the left or western wall into the last apartment of the series. Through the western wall of this apartment a doorway opened on the end of the ledge and the western cove. This principal entrance is shown in plate XLVIII. Its size is exceptional, it being about 6 feet high. A little below the top there is a single stick across it, and a similar contrivance was found in place in the openings in the tower, but it does not occur in the opening in the cross wall. The same feature is found in the modern pueblos, where the stick forms the support of a blanket draped to close the opening.

A little east of the doorway in the front wall there is a small opening near the ground, through which can be seen what appears to be a roof. It is but 2 feet above the ground, however, and very roughly constructed. It consists of a layer of cedar logs; above this a layer of small sticks, and above this again slabs of stone and mud. It occurs

BUREAU OF AMERICAN ETHNOLOGY

EASTERN COVE OF MUMMY CAVE

under a narrow room or passage, shown on the plan, and seems to have been the floor of that room rather than a roof of a space below.

Roofing or flooring beams project from the tower on three sides. They are all rounded and carefully selected or matched. Those of the lower story or first roof are 4½ inches in diameter, those of the story above about 3 inches, while those of the roof, which occur in pairs, are about 2½ inches. They all, except those of the lower story, project about 2 feet from the wall. All the beams are from 18 inches to 2 feet apart, and the roof is formed of canes or willow sticks less than half an inch in diameter laid very neatly in patterns. The work here is by far the best in any part of the canyon. The beams of the first floor are represented only by the ends which pass through the walls, the middle portion being gone.

The cliff wall forming one side of the rooms in the tower was coated with a wash of yellowish clay to correspond with the other sides. It shows bare rock at the points where the floors abutted against it. The roof of the second story or middle room was 10 inches thick, and the marks are on the same level as those of the rooms over the west of the tower. There are also beam holes in the third story about 4 feet above its floor, but extending only from the cliff out to its opening.

A singular feature occurs in the tower, which is difficult to explain. The upper part of the third-story room was coated in the interior with whitewash, which appears to have been carelessly applied. Small quantities struck the setback at the floor level and spattered over the wall below—that of the second-story room. In one case a considerable quantity of the whitewash struck the top of a beam in what would be the roof of the second story and scattered over the wall surface below it. It is therefore clear that at the time when the whitewash was applied, which was either at the time or subsequent to the habitation of the rooms, there was no floor to the third-story room nor roof to the second story. The stains of whitewash never go below the floor level of the second story.

The house remains in the eastern cove are partly shown in plate XLIX, which is from a photograph. The point of view is from the ledge in front of the tower. The ruins rest on a ledge in the back of the cove formed of débris well compacted and apparently consisting partly of sheep dung. The rooms are small, sometimes three deep against the back of the cove, and many of them could only have been used for storage. The principal structure is the western kiva, with its chimney-like attachments. This is described at length on pages 177, 179, 186, and 187. Adjoining it on the east is another kiva, part of whose wall is still two stories high, and clearly shown in the illustration. Some 50 or 60 feet to the east or southeast there is another circular structure, which apparently had no interior bench. The small semicircular structure shown on the plan and in the illustration, which rests against and is roofed by the rock, is a Navaho burial cist, and another of these cists, of large size, occurs west of the principal kiva; but the ruin as a whole contains much less evidence of Navaho work than those farther down the canyon.

Many of the walls are built entirely of small pieces of stone, not more than 3 or 4 inches long by 2 inches wide and half an inch to an inch and a half thick. This construction is especially noticeable in inner walls. The joints are carefully plastered, evidently with the hand, but the mud is seldom allowed to cover the stone. It appears to have been applied externally, in pellets about the size of a walnut. The general thickness of walls is about 15 inches, although on the intermediate ledge they are over 2 feet, but some of the less important walls consist of a single layer, 6 to 8 inches thick. Walls are sometimes seen here supported by vertical timbers incorporated in them after the manner later described at some length. Ends of logs project here and there from the débris on the slope, but probably many of them are the débris of roofs.

The peculiar and anomalous features presented by the remains on the intermediate ledge seem to require some explanation. This portion of the ruin is not only different from the other portions, but different also from anything else in the canyon, and the difference is not one of degree only. Doubtless systematic excavation in the various parts of the ruin would afford an explanation. In the absence of such work we can only speculate on the problem.

The occurrence of two chimney-like shafts in connection with the rectangular rooms west of the tower is significant. Nowhere else in the canyons, except in the Casa Blanca ruin, do these structures occur, so far as known, except in connection with circular kivas. As regards the ruin named, it is almost certain that it was occupied in the historic period, probably in the seventeenth century.

The division of the ruin into three separate parts, the absence of kivas in the western cove, and the method of access to that portion all attract attention. If there were monks or other Spaniards in the settlement, the explanation would be plain; they and those of the natives allied with them would occupy the central ledge, and the anomalous features would be natural under the circumstances. Such a hypothesis would explain also the source of the many unaboriginal features which are found in other parts of the canyon, but there is no direct evidence to support it. It should be mentioned, however, that the walls here rest on about half an inch of substance which resembles compacted sheep dung. If the substance is really such, the walls must have been built within the historic period.

At the point marked 48 on the map there is a ruin which resembles somewhat in its location an example previously described (page 98). It is situated in a cove in a jutting point of rock, forming part of the talus slope, and is about 20 feet above the bottom, which it overlooks. Figure 17 shows the character of the site, and figure 18 is a ground plan. At the back of the cove a row of small rooms, five or six in number, was built against the rock. In front of these there were two kivas and perhaps other rooms. Only fragments of these now remain, but it can still be seen that both kivas had interior

Fig. 17—Ruin in a rock cove.

benches, and that the western one has been plastered with several successive coats—at least four. There are no pictographs on the back wall, and but little staining by smoke. The masonry is rather rough, consisting of large stones, pretty well chinked with small spawls.

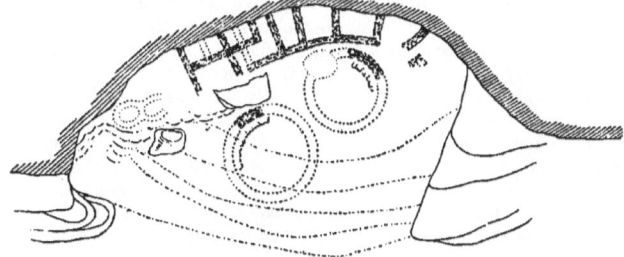

Fig. 18—Ground plan of a ruin in a rock cove.

Some of the walls were plastered. The western end of the ruin has been partially restored by the Navaho and used for burial cists, and other cists have been built on the site independent of the old walls, as shown on the plan. Figure 19 is a ground plan of a ruin on a ledge near the mouth of Del Muerto, at the point marked 15 on the map. It is situated at the back of a considerable bay, directly opposite a large rock at the mouth of Del Muerto, and overlooked the whole of the bottom land in the bay. The houses were built on a bench or ledge, about 30 feet wide, overhung by the cliff above and dropping down almost vertically to the bottom land, about 40 feet below, but on the east access to the bench was easy by a slope of talus extending up to it. The site was covered with bowlders, and walls have been built over and under them. The masonry is good, and was composed of larger stones than usual, carefully chinked with spalls, the work being well done.

There were but 10 rooms on the ground, in addition to one circular kiva; some of these rooms are too small for habitation, and one of them appears to have been a rectangular kiva. On the same bench, about 100 feet westward, however, there are traces of other rooms, the walls of which were very thin. The cliffs back of the ruin and for 200 feet west of it are covered with pictographs in white and colors.

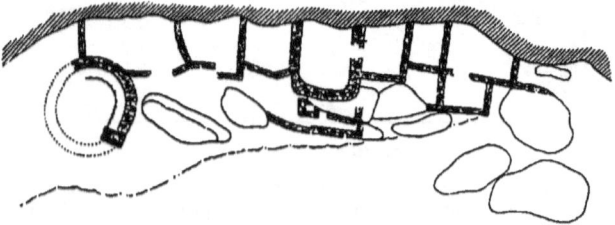

Fig. 19—Ground plan of a ruin on a ledge.

Near the center of that portion of the ruin shown on the ground plan there is a large room which may have been a rectangular kiva. The walls are over 2 feet thick in the first story, diminishing at the roof level by a step or setback to the ordinary thickness of about a foot. These walls, as usual in such structures, were about 2 feet thick; they are slightly curved, the front wall markedly so, and the interior corners are well rounded. No reason for this curvature is apparent, and it is certainly not dictated by the occurrence of the rock over which the wall is built, as only the point of this rock comes through the wall in the western side of the front wall. There may have been an opening into the room through the eastern wall connecting it with the room on that side, as the masonry is there broken down; but this is doubtful, as the eastern room itself has no exterior opening. It is more probable that the large room was entered through the roof, for the thin wall of the second story shows in front one side of a well-finished doorway.

Just outside of the heavy front wall there is a round hole in the ground, the remains of a vertical shaft connected with the interior of the room. The hole is about a foot in diameter, and is neatly plastered inside, and appears to have been a chimney or a chimney-like structure such as occur in connection with the kivas in other ruins. It will later be discussed in detail.

The circular kiva occupies the western end of that part of the room shown in the plan. It was 15 feet in diameter, and is exceptionally well built. The wall is standing for about half of its circumference, and was so neatly finished that the interior coating of plaster was apparently omitted. There are no traces of inclosing rectangular walls; the thickness of the kiva walls and the exceptionally large stones used in parts of it suggest that the kiva stood alone. So far as the walls remain standing, an interior bench can be traced, about 2 feet wide and 6 feet below the top of the outside wall. On the southeastern side, in the interior, there is a buttress or projection, which terminates the bench at this point.

The walls between the rectangular room described and the circular kiva are thin and very irregularly laid out. In front of the rectangular room and on the edge of the bench, which is here but a few feet above the talus, a rather heavy wall has been built over the top of a rock,

FIG. 20—Ground plan of ruin No. 31, Canyon de Chelly.

and inside or to the north of it another wall has been placed, hardly 2 feet distant. These walls are connected at the eastern end by a thin cross wall, now but slightly above the ground surface and notched like a doorway. Below the notch a slab of stone has been placed and was apparently used as a step. The purpose of these walls is not clear, but they may have constituted an entrance or passageway to the village. If so, we have here a very efficient defensive expedient and a decided anomaly in cliff-village architecture.

At the point marked 31 on the map there is a small ruin on a ledge about 150 feet above the bottom and difficult of access. The site overlooks considerable areas of bottom land on both sides of the canyon, and was probably connected with and formed part of a larger ruin on the same ledge and east of it, which will next be described. On this site there are remains of half a dozen rooms or more and of one circular kiva, which was 20 feet in diameter. (See ground plan, figure 20.) The site has been much filled up, and the kiva appears as a cylindrical depression, flush with the ground outside, but 3 to 5 feet deep inside. The walls are rather thin and smoothly plastered inside. On the south

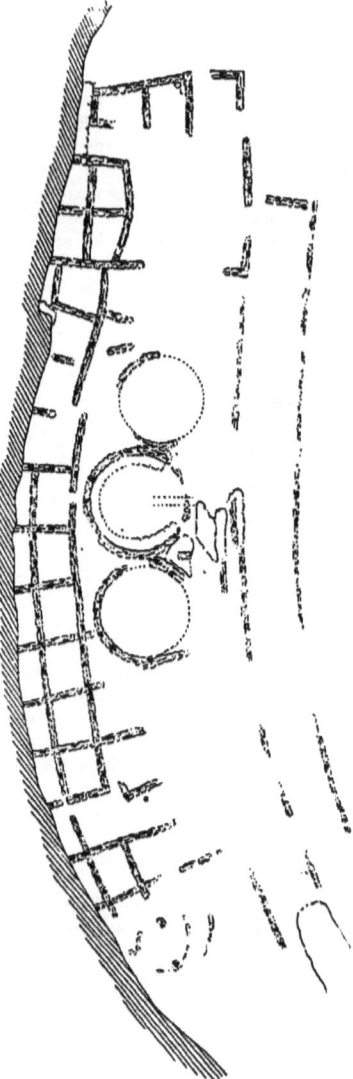

FIG. 21—Ground plan of ruin No. 22, Canyon de Chelly.

side there is an opening extending down to the floor level and opening directly on the sharply sloping rock. This feature will later be discussed at some length. The walls to the west of the kiva are still 14 or 15 feet high, showing two stories, and were well constructed and smoothly plastered. The interior of the kiva shows a number of successive coats of plastering—at least eight.

Immediately above the last-mentioned ruin, and on the same ledge, occur the remains of a large settlement, shown in plan in figure 21. It will be noticed that here, as in some of the previous examples described, the general arrangement consists of a row of rooms against the cliff, with the kivas in front. There were at least 17 rooms in line, and there may have been as many as 30 to 50 rectangular rooms in the village, scattered over an area nearly 200 feet long by 65 feet wide, but not all of this area was covered. Three kivas are still clearly shown.

This ruin is especially interesting on account of the site it occupies. The walls were placed on sharply sloping rock and in some cases on loose débris, and numerous expedients were resorted to to prevent them from slipping down the slope. The fact that these expedients were not successful makes them more interesting. Upright logs were inclosed in the walls and anchored in holes drilled in the rock below; horizontal logs were built into the masonry as ties and placed below it, and heavy retaining walls were erected. These constructive expedients will later be discussed at greater length.

The whole slope is more or less covered with débris, and there is no doubt that this was at one time a considerable settlement. The cliff walls near the east end show traces of two stories, and in one place of three stories, which formerly rested against them. Moreover, the number of successive coats of plaster in the kiva shows an extended occupancy, an inference which is further supported by the variety of expedients which were adopted to hold the walls in place.

The marked irregularity of the five eastern rooms as compared with the regular series west of them will be noticed on the plan. These eastern rooms must have been added at a period subsequent to the completion of the others. The marks of a second and third story occur on the cliff back of this cluster, and there is no doubt that it was an important part of the settlement. West of the area shown on the plan traces of walls occur on the slope and among the débris for a distance of over 100 feet.

Parts of three kivas can now be seen on the ground, and this was probably the total number in the settlement. The fronts of all of them have fallen out, notwithstanding various expedients that were employed to hold them in place. The western wall of the western kiva is part of the rectangular system and was apparently in place before the kiva was built. A triangular block which formed the junction in front of this kiva and the central one has slipped down and new walls were afterward built to restore the kivas to their original shape. The central kiva has an interior bench, which was, however, added after the structure was completed, and in fact after the front had been replaced. The second falling off of the front has left a fine section of the wall, and the changes which have taken place are plainly shown in it.

That the interior bench was added long after the original kiva had been completed and occupied is shown by the occurrence between it and the wall of nearly an inch of plaster composed of separate coatings, each smoke-blackened, varying from the thickness of a piece of heavy paper up to an eighth of an inch or more. If one of these coatings were added each year, twelve or fifteen years at least must have elapsed between the building of the kiva and the construction of the interior bench. The original floor of the kiva was composed of a layer of mud mortar about an inch thick, and extends through under the bench, the top of which is about 3 feet above it. Under this floor there is a straight wall at right angles to the cliff and extending some 4 feet toward the center of the kiva; what is left of it is just under the floor level.

There is a suggestion in this that the site of the kiva was originally occupied by rectangular rooms, and there is a further suggestion, in the end sections referred to, that the kiva had at some period fallen into decay and was subsequently rebuilt. All this occurred before the first falling out of the front.

The section shows that the original walls were not so thick as the present ones, and that there was formerly a slight setback in the wall of 2½ or 3 inches at the level of the present bench, reducing the thickness of the wall by that amount. The original outside wall on the east extends only 6 inches above this setback. The upper portion of the exterior wall was added at the same time that the bench was constructed and is the same thickness as the lower part of the original wall. Figure 22 will make clear the changes which have taken place.

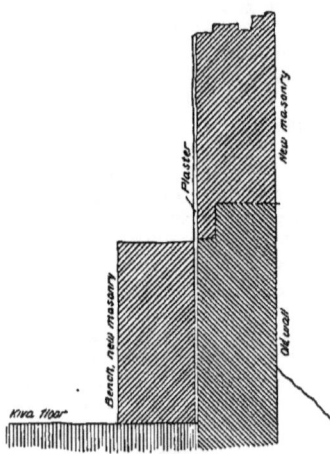

Fig. 22—Section of a kiva wall.

There was a recess of some kind in the original wall on the east and a similar one on the west side, but they have been filled up by the later additions. The upright logs which were built into the masonry are incorporated in the older walls. Under the floor, and apparently under the walls themselves, there is a layer nearly a foot thick of loose débris consisting of cornstalks, corn leaves, ashes, and loose dirt. The floor of the east circular room, which still covers about half the interior, rests similarly on a layer of ashes. The expedients employed to hold the front walls of these kivas in place are later discussed at some length.

Figure 23 shows the character of site occupied by a village ruin of some size situated in the first cove in the cliff wall below the mouth of Canyon del Muerto. The cliff here is about 300 feet high and the ruin is located on a ledge in a cove about 70 feet above the stream bed. Although seemingly very difficult to reach, the ruin is of comparatively easy access without artificial aid. The cavity was caused apparently by the occurrence of a pocket of material softer than that about it, and this softer material has weathered out, showing very strongly the lines of cross bedding, which, in the massive rock on either side, have been almost entirely obliterated. The strata are inclined at an angle and the edges project from a few inches to about a foot, forming a series of little benches tilted up at an angle of about 45 degrees. By the exercise of some agility, one can ascend along these benches. About half-way between the site of the ruin and the stream bed there is a narrow horizontal bench, and again halfway between this bench and the ruin there is another, about 55 feet above the stream. Access to the ruins is greatly facilitated by these intermediate ledges.

The bench on which the ruin occurs is about 250 feet long and generally about 20 feet wide, the surface being almost flat. There are structures on the extreme northern and on the extreme southern ends, but a considerable part of the intermediate area was not occupied. Reference to the ground plan (figure 24) will show that most of the buildings occur on the northern half of the ledge, which was fairly

FIG. 23—Ruin No. 10 on a ledge in a cove.

well filled by them. Many of the walls in this portion are apparently underlaid by a foot or more of ashes, sheep dung, domestic refuse, cornhusks, etc.

The room which is shown in the center of the plan, at the southern end of the main group, stood alone and was the largest rectangular room in the village. It covered an area 15 feet by 9 feet inside the walls, which are now 5 or 6 feet high. The masonry is very good, although chinking with spalls was but slightly employed to finish the exterior; inside it is more apparent. The western wall was built over the edge of the sloping rock forming the back of the cove, as shown on the plan, and this rock projects below the wall into the room. There were apparently no openings in the walls, except some very small ones on the

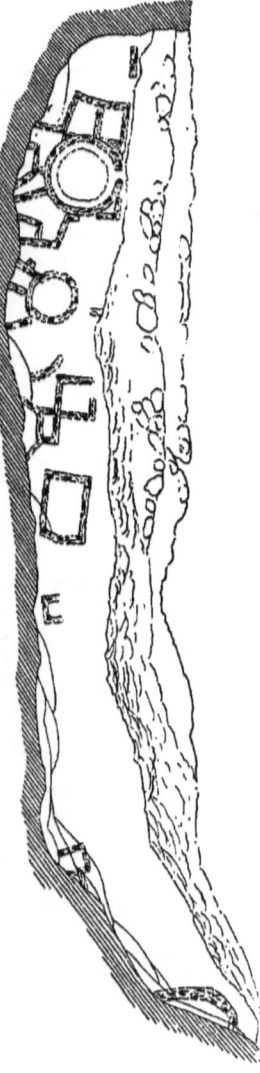

FIG. 21—Ground plan of ruin No. 10.

eastern side, near the floor level. In the southern wall a piece of rough timber was inlaid in the masonry, about 5 feet above the floor, flush with the wall inside and extending nearly through it. This piece of timber was crooked and its bend determined the wall line, which is bowed outward, as shown on the ground plan. This feature will be discussed later.

There were two circular kivas in the village, one of which was unusually small, being only about 10 feet in diameter north and south; the east-and-west diameter is a trifle smaller. There was apparently no bench in the interior, but on the western or northwestern side there is a bench-like recess of about a foot which occupies 7 feet of the circumference. The whole interior was covered with a number of washes of clay, applied one over another, forming a coating now nearly three-quarters of an inch thick. This is cracked and peeled off in places, and in the section eighteen coats, generally about one thirty-second of an inch thick, may be counted. Each coat or plastering is defined by a film of smoke-blackened surface.

On a level about 2 feet above the bench and about 5 feet above the present ground surface, there seems to have been some kind of roof. The stones here project into the interior slightly beyond the wall surface, and the plaster seems to curve inward. This point or level is from 6 to 18 inches below the top of the wall, and here there are remains of occasional small sticks, about an inch in diameter, which projected into the kiva. They are irregularly disposed and probably had no connection with the roof, but there are no traces of heavier timbers above them. In the interior a white band with points completely encircled the kiva. The top of this band is about a foot above the present ground surface and about 18 inches below the bench on the western side. It is illustrated in figure 72.

The exterior wall of the kiva was very roughly laid up, and some of the lower stones were set on edge, which is rather an anomalous feature. There is no evidence that the structure was ever inclosed in rectangular walls, as was the usual custom; in fact, the occurrence of other walls near it would apparently preclude such an arrangement. The wall which runs north or northwest from the kiva, joining it to the cliff wall behind, is pierced by a doorway some feet above the ground, and in front of or below this doorway there is a buttress or step of solid masonry, shown on the plan. There was apparently an open space between this doorway and the next wall to the north. The room entered through the doorway was very small, and its roof, formed by the overhanging cliff, is much blackened by smoke.

The main or north kiva was 15 feet in diameter on the floor, with a bench a foot wide extending around it. The external diameter is over 20 feet. The interior was decorated by bands and dots in white, which are described at length in another place (page 178). The roof was $5\frac{1}{2}$ feet above the bench, and there is a suggestion that it rested on a series of beams extending north and south, but this is not certain.

On the southeastern side, at the point where the kiva comes nearest the edge of the cliff, there was a narrow opening or doorway not more than 15 inches wide. This was the only entrance to the interior, except through the roof, and it opens directly on the edge of the cliff, so that it is very difficult, although not impossible, to pass it. In front of the opening a little platform was built on the sloping edge of the cliff, as though entrance was had from the lower bench by artificial means, but it is more probable that this feature is all that remains of a chimney-like structure.

Above this kiva there was apparently a living room, the walls of which, where they still remain on the north and west sides, were approximately straight, but the corners were rounded. The roof was formed by the overhanging cliff and the interior walls were white-washed. The kiva walls were about 18 inches thick, but on the west side, in the small room between the kiva and the cliff, the masonry is much heavier, the lower part extending into the room a foot farther than the upper. This is caused by the wall of the second-story room above setting in toward the east or center of the kiva. This upper wall was supported by a beam, part of which is still in place. The small room behind is much blackened by smoke.

The exterior wall of the main kiva on the northwest side is very rough. On the northeast and southeast, however, it is covered by straight walls which are well finished. The western end of the north wall is joined to the exterior circular wall of the kiva, at the point shown on the plan, by a short flying wall whose purpose is not clear. It extends to what may have been the roof of the kiva, but underneath it is open. The triangular cavity formed by it is too small to permit the passage of a person, and was available only from the second story.

The site of these ruins commands an extensive prospect, including several small areas of good bottom land, one of which lies directly in front of it; but the number of other ruins in the cove suggests that there was once a much larger area of bottom land here, and this suggestion is supported by the presence of several large cottonwood trees, now standing out in the midst of the sand, in the bed of the stream, where these trees never grow. Some of these trees are not yet entirely dead, indicating that the change in the bed of the stream was a recent one. Against the foot of the talus, just above the ruin, there is a narrow strip of bottom land, about 3 feet above the stream bed, and on it a single tree, still alive, but inclined at an angle. In the stream bed, above and below the ruin, there are large trees, of which only one or a few branches are still alive. The position of the cove with reference to the stream bed made the bottom lands here especially subject to erosion when the stream assumed its present channel and they were gradually worn away.

The western end of the ledge was occupied by a structure whose use at first sight is not apparent. The wall, as shown on the plan, is curved, very thick and heavy, and built partly over the sloping rock forming the back of the cave. The front wall is 3 feet thick, and its top, now level, is about 5 feet above a narrow bench in front of it. There is no doorway or other opening into it, and access into its interior was had over the steep sloping rock to the north by means of hand-holes in the rock. These are shown in plate L. The interior appears to have been plastered.

This structure measures 15 by 5 feet inside, there being no wall on the north, as the east wall merges into the sloping rock. The foot-holes in the rock, before referred to, are at this end, nearest the village, and appear to be in several series. The structure is so situated that the sun shines on it only a few hours each day, and it seems more than probable that it was a reservoir. The bed of the stream, the channel followed in low water, sweeps against the base of the cliff below this point, and by carrying water 20 feet it would be directly beneath and about 50 feet below it. Finally, the cliff wall above this point is decorated with pictographs of tadpoles and other water symbols in common use among the pueblos, and these do not occur elsewhere on this site. In the southwestern corner of the structure, near the bottom, there was an opening about 18 inches high, which was carefully filled up from the inside and plastered. This may have been an outlet by which the water was discharged when the reservoir was cleaned out. The wall has caved in slightly above it. The mud mortar used in building this structure and the other walls was necessarily brought from below.

RESERVOIR IN RUIN No. 10

About 25 feet east of the reservoir there are remains of a small single room, rectangular, with a circular addition, shown on the ground plan. The walls are well chinked and well constructed, the mud mortar being used when about the consistency of modeling clay. In front of this room, about 5 feet distant and on the edge of the sloping rock, a hole has been pecked into the solid rock of the ledge. This hole is 12 inches wide on top, slightly tapering, 10 inches deep on the upper side, and 4 inches on the lower. Twelve feet to the northeast there is a similar hole, and below it, distant 10 inches, another, and beyond this others, distributed generally along the foot of the sloping rock forming the back of the ledge, but sometimes farther out on the flat floor. Probably these holes mark the sites of upright posts supporting a drying scaffold or frame, the horizontal poles of which extended backward to the wall of the cliff.

Fig. 25—Oven-like structure in ruin No. 10.

Near the center of the ledge, at the point shown on the plan, there are some remains which strongly suggest the Mexican oven. The bed rock, which is here nearly flat, was removed to a depth of about 4 inches over a rectangular area measuring 4 feet north and south by 3½ feet. There were natural fissures in the rock on the north and west sides which left clean edges. The southern edge appears to have been smashed off with a rock. The eastern side required no dressing, as it was at a slightly lower level, and it was to reach this level that the rock was removed. In the rectangular space described there was a circular, dome shape structure, about 3 feet in diameter, composed of mud and sticks, with a scant admixture of small stones. This is shown in figure 25, and in plan in figure 26. The walls were about 3 inches thick, and from their slope the structure could not have been over 3 feet high. The mud which composed the walls was held together by thin sticks or branches, incorporated in it and carved with the wall—apparently some kind of a vine twisted together and incorporated bodily. On the edge of the rectangular space there is a drilled hole, 3 inches in diameter, shown in the illustration. Three feet to the south there is another, 6 inches in diameter.

If this structure was a dome-shape oven, and it is difficult to imagine it anything else, its occurrence here is important. It is well known that the dome-shape oven, which is very common in all the pueblos, in some villages being numbered by hundreds, is not an aboriginal feature, but was borrowed outright from the Mexicans. If the structure above described was an oven, it is clear evidence of the occupancy of these ruins within the historic period—it might almost be said within the last century. No other structure of the kind was found in the canyon, however, and it should be stated that the ovens of the pueblos are as a rule rather larger in size than this and usually constructed of small stones and mud—sometimes of regular masonry plastered. There is a sugges-

Fig. 26—Plan of oven-like structure.

tion here, which is further borne out by the chimney-like structures to be discussed later, that only the idea of these structures was brought here, without detailed knowledge of how to carry it out—as if, for example, they were built by novices from description only.

Figure 27 is the ground plan of a small village ruin situated at the mouth of Del Muerto at the point marked 16 on the map. The site, which is an excellent one, but rather difficult of access, overlooks the bottom land at the junction of the canyons and a long strip on the opposite side, together with a considerable area above. The approach is over smooth sandstone inclined at such an angle as to make it difficult to maintain a footing, but the ruin can be reached without artificial aid.

The village was not of large extent and contained but one kiva, but the walls were well constructed and the masonry throughout is exceptionally good. The exterior wall of the western rooms was constructed of small stones neatly laid. The eastern room of the two was built after the other, and entrance was had by an almost square opening 2 feet from the ground. To facilitate ingress, a notch was dug in the wall about 8 inches from the ground. There was no communication between the rooms, the western room being entered by a small doorway on the western side, about 8 inches from the ground, 3 feet high and 14 inches wide. There was no plastering in the interior of these rooms.

The kiva is 15 feet in diameter on the floor, and about 23 feet in its exterior diameter. The walls are 3 feet thick above the bench level and 4 feet

SMALL VILLAGE, RUIN No. 16, CANYON DE CHELLY

thick below it. The interior was plastered with a number of successive coats, probably four or five in all; but although the wall is still standing to a height of 4 feet or more above the bench, there are gaps on the eastern and western sides which render it impossible to say whether doorways were there or not. The eastern break exposes the western side of the inclosing wall, which is smoothly finished as though there were originally a recess here. There are rectangular inclosing walls on the east and south; the northern side was formed by the cliff against which the kiva rests, while on the west there are no traces of an inclosing wall. The triangular spaces formed by the inclosing walls on the northeast and southeast sides of the kiva were not filled up in the customary manner, but appear to have been preserved as storerooms. The southeastern space was connected with the kiva by a narrow doorway, shown in the plan, and another doorway, completely sealed, led from this space into the room adjoining on the east. The latter doorway had not been used for a long time prior to the abandonment of the ruin,

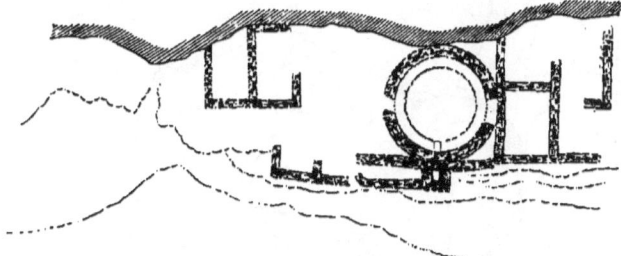

and its opening into the rectangular room was carefully concealed from that side by several successive coats of plaster.

On the south side of the kiva and outside the rectangular wall is a square buttress or chimney-like construction, 4 by 3 feet, inclosing a shaft 10 by 5 inches. This feature will be discussed in another place. It was added after the wall was completed, and embedded in it, about a foot from the ground, is a heavy beam about 5 inches in diameter. Plate LI, which shows the whole front of the village, will make this feature clear. The beam projects from the kiva wall at or under the floor level, and seems to have no reference to the shaft, which is, however, shouldered to accommodate it. Similar beams project from the walls to the east, about 8 inches above the bed rock.

In the room east of the kiva no doorway was found. The walls are still intact to a minimum height of 6 feet from the floor, except in the southeast corner, where they are 3 feet. The opening described, which occurs in the southwest corner of the room, was 4 feet from the floor; and in the southeast corner, where the wall is broken down, there now

16 ETH——9

are remains of one side of a similar opening on the same level. No stains of smoke are found on the exterior coat of plaster in this room, but the coats underneath were much blackened. The room north of the one described, and adjoining the kiva, was also without a doorway, unless it existed in the northeast corner, next the cliff, where no trace of walls now remains. The walls of this room, now 6 feet high, were plastered and show old smoke stains. The wall on the western side of the kiva is very rough, as though at one time another wall existed outside of it. This is shown in plate LII, which shows also the débris, consisting of ashes, sheep dung, and refuse, well compacted, upon which the wall rests.

FIG. 28—Ruins on a large rock.

West of the kiva and on the extreme edge of the cliff are the remains of two small apartments, a trifle below the surface of the ledge and with a 3-foot wall on the south. These are too small for habitations, and were used probably for the storage of corn. About 100 feet west of the group described, on the same bench, there are remains of a large room, divided into two, and of quite rough construction. It contains several Navaho dead and may be of Navaho origin.

A type of site which is abundant in the San Juan country and is found in other regions, but is very rare in this, is shown in figure 28.

WALLS RESTING ON REFUSE IN RUIN No. 16

This example, which occurs in the upper part of Del Muerto, is the only one of its kind in the canyons. A large mass of rock, smoothed and rounded by atmospheric erosion, but still connected with the cliff at one point, juts out into the bottom, a large area of which is commanded by it. At three different levels there are remains of rooms, the group on the summit being the largest. It is doubtful whether any of these remains represent permanent villages, but it is possible that the uppermost one did. It is therefore included in this place.

At the point marked 49 on the map there is a ruin or group of ruins which presents some anomalous features. Figure 29 shows in detail the distribution of the remains. The rooms were located on narrow benches in the cliff, the principal part on a high, narrow bench, 40 or 50 feet above the top of the talus and over 300 feet above the canyon bottom. Access to the upper ledge from the top of the talus is exceedingly difficult, requiring a climb over almost vertical rock for 40 feet. Above the ledge there is massive sandstone, but below it for 100 feet or more there is an area of cross bedding, and the rock has an almost vertical cleavage,

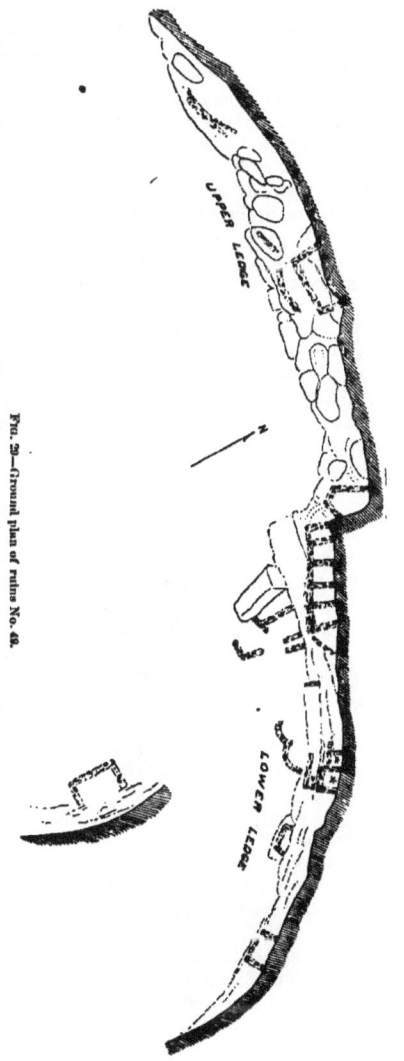

FIG. 29—Ground plan of ruins No. 48

apparently standing upright in thin slabs 2 to 6 inches thick. Access was had by aid of the rough projections of the slabs, aided where necessary by hand and foot holes pecked in the rock. At several places little platforms of masonry have been built.

At the northern end of the upper ledge there are five small cells occupying its whole width, and whose front wall follows the winding ledge. The walls are about 5 feet high, and their tops bear the marks of the poles which carried the roof. There are no exterior openings, nor is there any evidence of a means of communication between the rooms; but in the second room from the south two stones project from the wall inside, near the southeastern corner, forming rude steps, doubtless to a trapdoor in the roof. These cells could hardly have been used as habitations. The floors are covered with many lumps of clay, which apparently formed part of the roof.

To the south of this cluster of cells there was a large room of irregular shape on a level about 8 feet higher. The remainder of the ledge, which is about on the same level as this large room, is almost covered with large bowlders, but at several points on it other remains of walls occur. The largest room of all was near its center. It was built against the cliff, which formed one of its sides, and measured about 16 by 6 feet. There are no evidences of any partitions or roof, the latter probably being formed by the overhanging rock. As the room was built partly on the sloping rock, the floor is very uneven. It could hardly have been used as a habitation, but may have been employed for the storage of water.

The southern end of the lower ledge merges into the head of the talus, the northern part drops down by a sharply sloping and in places an almost vertical wall of about 30 feet; thence it descends to the bottom by a long slope of bare rock, generally passable on foot. The lower ledge is about 50 feet above the upper. Upon it are scattered the remains of a few rooms of the same general character as those above, but smaller. Many of these have been utilized for modern Navaho burials, and perhaps some of them were constructed for that purpose. If these rooms were used as habitations, it must have been under very peculiar circumstances; moreover, the site is hardly suited . for such a purpose, having the sunshine less than half of the day. In this respect it is anomalous.

At the southern end of the ledge there is a large angular bowlder, one edge of which rests against the cliff wall and is free from the ground. Under this the walls of a small room can be seen. The cliff formed one side of the room and the bowlder acted as a roof. On the extreme northern end of the ledge, 200 feet distant from the nearest room, there are remains of a structure standing alone. The masonry is much rougher than that of the other rooms, and, although the walls are now about 6 feet high, there is no evidence of any doorway or opening into the room.

On the surface of the sloping rock, at this point nearly flat, there are traces of a circular kiva 18 or 20 feet in diameter. These traces occur at a point about midway between the southern and northern ends of the lower ledge and some 30 feet below it. The cliff walls, both of the lower and upper ledges, are covered with pictographs in white, red, and yellow.

Fig. 30—Ruin on an almost inaccessible site.

The location and character of this site and the character of the remains suggest that most if not all of the rooms which can now be traced were used for storage only. For this purpose the site is well adapted. But the remains of the circular kiva at the foot of the lower ledge show plainly that there were at one time some habitations here. Doubtless these were located on the smooth rock at the foot of the cliff, and the disappearance of all traces of walls may be due to the subsequent use of the material by the Navaho for the construction of burial cists, in which the site abounds. There still remains on the ground a fair amount of broken stone, suitable for building, but no lines of wall are now traceable.

Figure 30 shows one of the most inaccessible sites in the canyon. It occurs at the point marked 62 on the map, where there is a narrow ledge nearly 400 feet above the stream. The approach is over bare rock, sharply sloping, but passable at two points by an active man accustomed to climbing. Both of these points are near the western or left-hand end of the ruin; toward the right the rock becomes vertical. Immediately below this ruin there are the remains of a large settlement on a low spur near the stream, now much obliterated, and

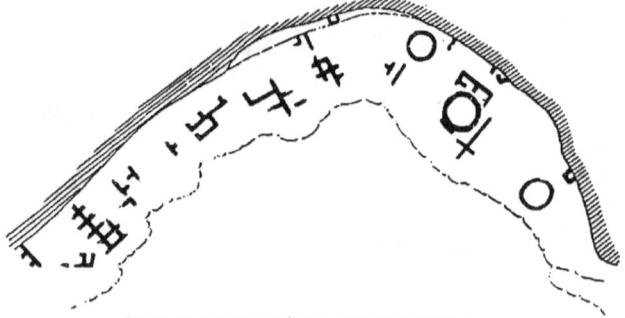

FIG. 31—Ground plan of a large ruin in Canyon del Muerto.

above and below it on suitable sites there were a number of small settlements which may have been connected with it.

There were a number of rooms scattered along the ledge which appear to have been used as habitations. The overhanging cliff is so close that in a number of cases it formed the roof of the room, and the whole site was an inconvenient and dangerous one. The rooms on the east rest on a large block which has split off from the wall since the walls were built, and now hangs apparently ready to drop at any moment.

At the time this site was inhabited access was had over the smooth rounded rock on the west. Here hand and foot holes have been pecked in the steep places, but as the rock is much exposed to atmospheric erosion these holes are now almost obliterated. After ascending the rock the village was entered through a doorway in a wall of exceptional thickness, shown on the left of the drawing. The room which was entered through this doorway appears to have been placed at this point to command the entrance to the village. The wall is exceptionally heavy and was pierced with oblique loopholes commanding a narrow bench immediately in front of it. This appears to have been a purely defensive expedient, and as such is unique.

The site commands an extensive outlook over the canyon bottom, including several areas of cultivable land, and while it may have been occupied as a regular village, such occupancy could not have been long

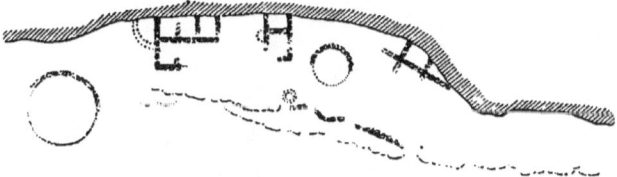

Fig. 32—Ground plan of a small ruin in Canyon del Muerto.

continued. Altogether the site and the character of the house remains are anomalous and doubtless resulted from anomalous conditions.

Figure 31 is a ground plan of a large ruin in Del Muerto. It occupied almost the whole available area of the ledge on which it is situated, and over 40 rooms can now be made out on the ground, in addition to 3 circular kivas. The settlement may have comprised between 80 and 100 rooms, which would accommodate 15 to 20 families. The size is very unusual, and the presence of but 3 kivas would indicate that the families were closely related. There are other examples of this character in the canyons, but not so large as the one illustrated.

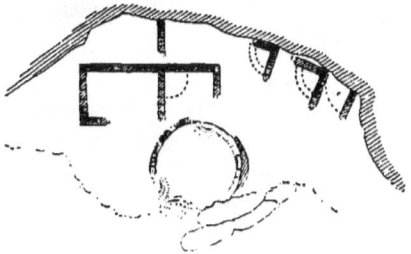

Fig. 33—Ground plan of a small ruin.

Figure 32 illustrates a type which is more common. Here we have the usual arrangement of rooms along the cliff, with a kiva in front of them. There were altogether not over 10 or 12 rooms, and they were probably occupied by one family. Figure 33 shows a kind rather more abundant than the last, and consisting like it of one circular kiva with rooms back of and between it and the cliff. Ruins of this type are generally well protected by an overhanging cliff. Figure 34 is another example, in which only three rectangular rooms can be made out. The site here is almost covered with large bowlders. All these examples occur in Del Muerto.

Figure 35 is a ground plan of a small ruin which occurs at the point marked 36 on the map. It is situated in a shallow cove at the head of the talus, 200 or 300 feet above the bottom, and is of comparatively

FIG. 34—Plan of a ruin of three rooms.

easy access. There is but a small amount of cultivable bottom land immediately below it, but it commands extensive areas on the opposite site of the canyon and in the lower part of a branch on that side. There are but few remains of rooms other than parts of two kivas, but there is no question that there was at one time a considerable number here. Both kivas had interior benches, and were of small size, plastered

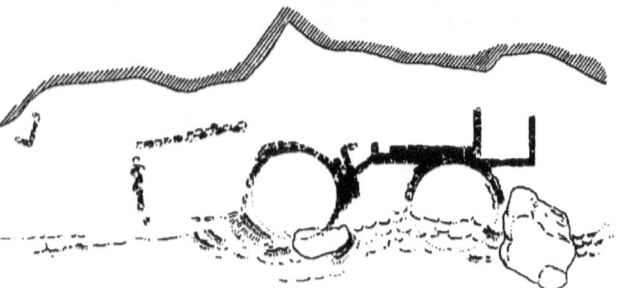

FIG. 35—Ground plan of a small ruin, with two kivas.

in the interior. The masonry is fair to good. On the highest point of the bowlder shown on the right of the plan there is a fragment of compacted sheep dung and soil, which is now 6 feet above the ground. It is all that remains of a layer of some thickness which must have been deposited when the surface was filled up to or nearly to the top of the rock. Possibly there was a wall outside and only the intermediate space was filled.

Figure 36 is the ground plan of a somewhat similar ruin which occurs at the point marked 44 on the map. It is situated on the top of the talus, against the cliff, and commands a fine outlook over the cultivable lands in the cove below it and on the canyon bottom proper. There are but few wall remains, but two kivas can still be made out. There is no ledge here, and the walls were built on loose débris of rocks and talus.

FIG. 36—Ground plan of a small ruin, No. 44.

The builders had some trouble in holding the walls in place, and only partly succeeded in doing so. About one-half of the principal kiva is standing, showing masonry composed of exceptionally large stones, roughly chinked. The other, or western kiva, was similarly constructed, and both had interior benches. The front of the western kiva fell out, the builders being unable to tie it or to hold it in place on its

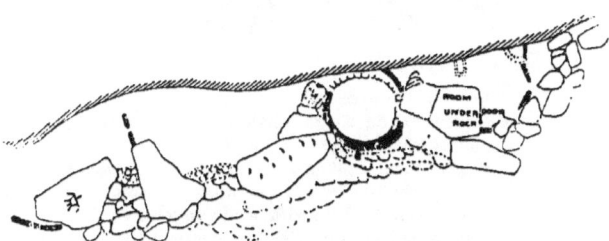

FIG. 37—Ground plan of a ruin on a rocky site.

loose foundation, and other walls were constructed inside of it, as shown on the plan. There were other walls outside the main kiva, apparently rectangular inclosing walls. This example is interesting because the masonry was constructed on a foundation of loose débris, not on bed rock, and the knowledge possessed by the builders was not sufficient to enable them to overcome the natural difficulties of the site.

Although ultimately the village had to be abandoned as a failure, it was certainly occupied for some years, and this occupancy suggests that there was some strong objection to the lower part of the canyon. It illustrates, moreover, the importance which was attached to a command or outlook over extensive cultivable areas, as to obtain such an outlook the builders were content to occupy even such an unsuitable site as the one described.

Figure 37 shows a small ruin similar to those described, but located on a site almost covered with large bowlders. The principal structure now remaining is a circular kiva, which, contrary to the usual plan, was placed close up against the cliff; possibly the cliff formed part of the back wall. Large bowlders so closely hemmed in the structure that there was neither space nor necessity for an inclosing wall. The kiva was benched for about half of its circumference.

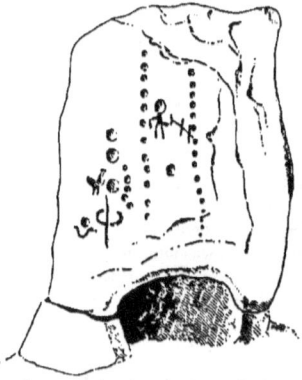

FIG. 38—Rock with cups and petroglyphs.

Under the large bowlder to the right of the kiva a complete room had been built, with a doorway of the usual type through the front wall. Scattered remnants of other walls may be seen here and there, but none show well-defined rooms. Petroglyphs are quite numerous, and one small bowlder to the left of and next to the kiva is covered with cups, dots, and carvings. It is shown in figure 38.

Figure 39 shows a ruin where the site was not so restricted. One well-defined room and two kivas still remain, and there are traces of other chambers. The main kiva formed part of a compact little group of rooms, of which it occupied the front, and appears to have been inclosed by a curved wall of rough construction. A curved inclosing wall is an anomalous feature, and it is not at all certain that it occurs here, as the wall is so much broken down that its lines can not now be clearly made out. Excavation would doubtless determine this, as the whole site has been much filled up with sand and loose earth.

The second kiva, which was about the same size as the first, was situated some little distance from the other, and on the outer edge of the little platform or bench on which the settlement was located. It still shows about half of its wall. The rectangular room near the main kiva still stands to a height of 3 and 4 feet. The wall nearest the kiva is pierced by a number of small openings, and by a neatly finished double-notched doorway, which is illustrated in another place (figure 67).

The whole front of the site has been filled up to a probable depth of several feet, and a number of Navaho burials have been made on it.

These are shown on the plan by shaded spots. Owing to the soft ground underneath, it was easier to excavate a hole and wall it up than to construct the regular surface cist, and the former plan was followed.

Although many of the sites are covered with bowlders and blocks of stone fallen from above, which often occur among and even over walls, close inspection generally shows that the walls were constructed after the rocks fell. There are two instances, however, which are doubtful, and in one (shown in figure 40) it appears that large blocks of rock have fallen since the walls were constructed. Such falls of rock are not uncommon now in the fall and winter months, when frost and seepage from the melting snow sometimes split off huge fragments.

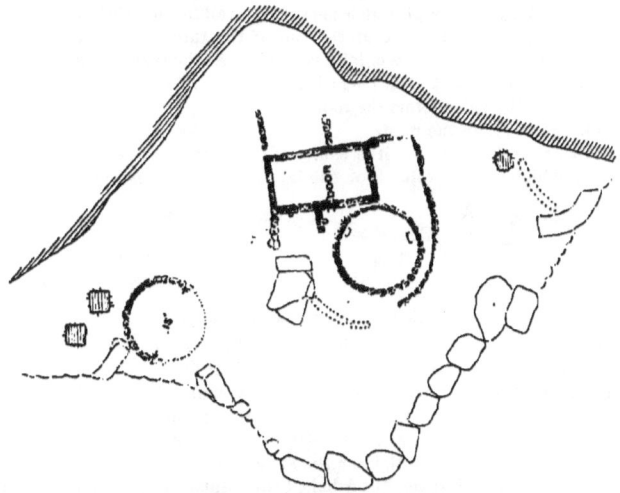

Fig 39—Ground plan of a ruin in Canyon de Chelly.

The site mentioned occurs at the point marked 47 on the map. It is in a cove under a mass of rock which juts out from the cliff, and is about 30 feet above the bottom, on the edge of a slope of loose rock which extends some distance above it. At the top of the talus, over 200 feet above, there is another ruin, which was probably only an outlook, as no trace of a kiva can be found, and it is possible that the lower site was connected with and formed part of the upper one. The lower site contained a circular kiva, only a small portion of which now remains, and the ground is covered with blocks of rock which must have fallen since the walls were built. They appear to have fallen quite recently. It can still be seen that the kiva had an interior bench, and that there was a room, or perhaps rooms, between it and the back of the cove; but beyond this nothing can now be made out.

There are many favorable sites in the branch canyons, but not many of them are occupied, possibly because in the upper parts of these canyons the bottom land is of small area and is sometimes rough, being composed of numerous small hillocks. The flat bottom lands of the canyon proper are much easier to cultivate, but the sites in the side canyons offered much better facilities for defense. Figure 41 shows the plan of a ruin which occurs at the point marked 69 on the map, on the western side of

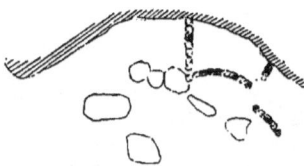

Fig. 40—Site showing recent fall of rock.

a branch canyon through which passes the trail to Fort Defiance. It is situated in a shallow cove at the top of the talus and overlooks an extensive area of fine bottom land below it. At the eastern end there is a single room about 10 feet long; its front wall extends up to the overhanging rock, which forms the roof of the room. A small cist has been built against it on the west.

About 60 feet west, on the same ledge, there are remains of other rooms which rested probably on the talus. Several rooms can be made

Fig. 41—Ruin No. 69, in a branch canyon.

out, but only one shows standing walls. This is on the western end, and the walls are now about 5 feet high. Four feet from the top of the wall there is a clear line of demarcation extending horizontally across it. Below this line the masonry consists of large flat slabs of rock laid in mud mortar, which was used nearly dry and stuffed into the cracks to some extent. Above the line the stones were carefully selected and the work was well done, the whole being finished by a thin coat of plaster. There is no opening in the lower part, but in the upper part there is a neatly finished doorway 3 feet high and slightly tapering. The bottom of this opening extends 2 inches below the line, and the lintel is composed of a large slab of stone a trifle wider than the thickness of the wall, but fitted flush on the outside.

Fig. 42—Ground plan of a small ruin in Canyon del Muerto.

On a bench about 100 feet higher than the ruin described there are two small rooms, extending up to the overhanging rock above them. These rooms, which may be of Navaho origin, were reached by means of a narrow ledge extending from the top of a slope of loose rock and débris about 300 yards to the southward, or up the canyon.

Figure 42 is a ground plan of a small ruin in Del Muerto in which the usual preponderance of rectangular rooms is illustrated. The site was restricted, but there is an apparent attempt to carry out the usual arrangement of a row of rooms against the cliff, with a kiva in front.

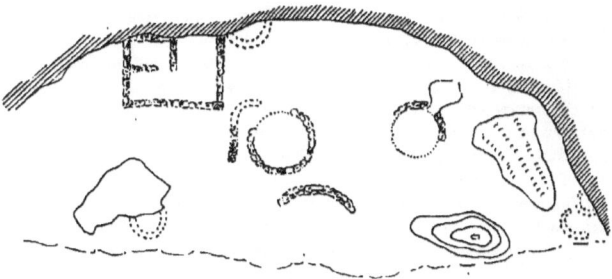

Fig. 43—Ground plan of a small ruin.

Probably only three of the rooms shown were used as habitations. The plan of the kiva, which occurs in the center, was somewhat marred by a large bowlder, which must have projected into it, but apparently no attempt was made to dress off the projecting point.

Figure 43 is the plan of a ruin located on a more open site. Only a few walls now remain, but there is no doubt that at one time more of

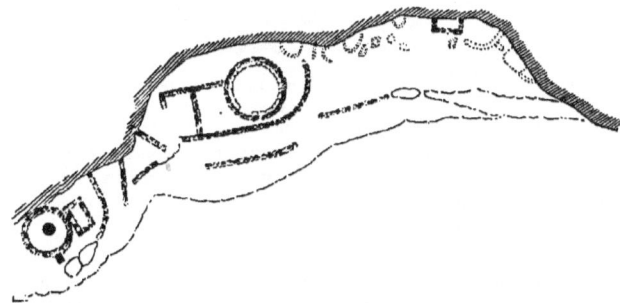

Fig. 44—Plan of a ruin with curved inclosing wall.

the site was covered than now appears. There are remains of two, and perhaps of three, circular kivas.

Figure 44 shows a ruin in which the plan is somewhat more elaborated. There are remains of several well-defined rooms, and two kivas are still fairly well preserved. The ledge is narrow and the rooms are stretched along it, with kivas at either end. That on the east was benched nearly all around its interior, and the outside inclosing wall, on the east, apparently follows the curve. An example in which this feature occurs has been mentioned above (page 138). It is very rare, but in this case the evidence is clearer than in the one previously described. The western kiva, somewhat smaller than the other, was also benched, and had an exterior shaft, like those mentioned above and later described at length.

Figure 45 is a plan of a small ruin of the same type, which occurs in the middle region of De Chelly. It occupies the site marked 34 on the map, and is situated in a niche in a deep cove, where the outlook is almost completely obscured by a large sand dune in front of it. It comprised one circular kiva and four rectangular rooms, but, contrary to the usual result, the latter are fairly well preserved, while the former is almost completely obliterated. This may be due to the use of the rectangular rooms as sites for Navaho burial cists, of which there are no fewer than six here, and possibly the kiva walls furnished the necessary building material for the construction of the cists. The old masonry is of good quality, the outside wall being

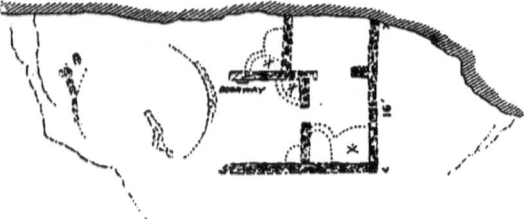

FIG. 45—Ground plan of ruin No. 34.

formed of selected stones of medium size, well laid and carefully chinked. Most of the walls were plastered inside. In a cleft in the rock to the right of this ruin there is a kind of cave, with foot-holes leading up the rock to it, and quite difficult of access. It formerly may have been used for storage, but at present contains only some remains of Navaho burials.

IV—CLIFF OUTLOOKS OR FARMING SHELTERS

Ruins comprised in the class of cliff outlooks, or farming shelters, are by far the most numerous in the canyon. They were located on various kinds of sites, but always with reference to some area of cultivable land which they overlooked, and seldom, if ever, was the site selected under the influence of the defensive motive. It is not to be understood that such motive was wholly absent; it may have been present in some cases, but the dominating motive was always convenience to some adjacent area of cultivable land.

The separation of this class of ruins from the preceding village ruins, while clear and definite enough in the main, is far from absolute. The sole criterion we have is the presence or absence of the kiva, as the sites occupied are essentially the same; but this test is in a general way sufficient. It is possible that in certain cases the kiva is so far obliterated, as to be no longer distinguishable, but the number of cases in which this might have occurred is comparatively small. The kivas, as a rule, were more solidly constructed than the other rooms, and, as the preceding ground plans show, sometimes survived when the rectangular rooms connected with them have entirely disappeared.

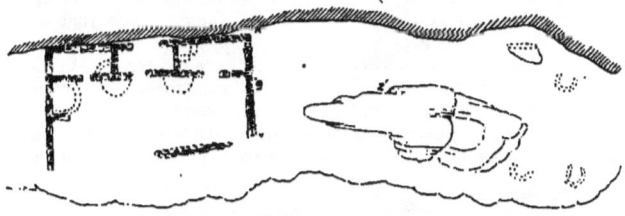

Fig. 46—Ground plan of cliff outlook No. 35.

Figure 46 is the plan of an outlook in the same cove as the last example of village ruin illustrated, and only 200 or 300 yards south of it. It may have been connected with that ruin, but could not in itself have been a village, as there are no traces of a kiva on the site, and hardly room enough for one on the bench proper. At the extreme northern end there are traces of walls on the rocks at a lower level.

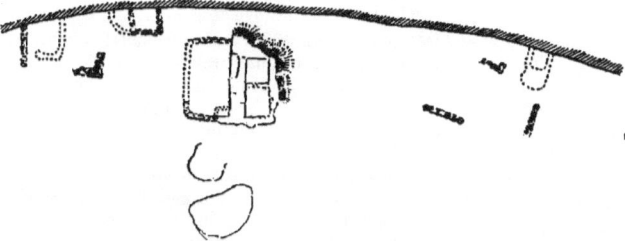

Fig. 47—Plan of a cliff outlook.

The walls which were at right angles to the cliff were not carried back to it after the usual manner, but stopped about 3 feet from it, and the rooms were closed by a back wall running parallel to the cliff, and about 3 feet from it. This wall rises to a height of about 4 feet before it meets the overhanging cliff, and consequently there is a long narrow passageway, about 3 feet high and 3 feet wide on the bottom, between it and the cliff. A small man might wriggle through, but with difficulty.

The ruin commands a fine outlook over the cove. The masonry is good, being composed of selected stone well chinked with small spalls, and sometimes with bits of clay pressed in with the fingers.

Figure 47 shows a ruin located at the point marked 37 on the map. There is a high slope of talus here, the top of which is flat and of considerable area.

The ruin is invisible from below in its present condition, but the site commands a fine outlook over several considerable areas of bottom land. The walls are now much obliterated and worked over by the Navaho, but the remains are scattered over quite an extensive area and may have been at one time an extensive settlement; however, no traces of a kiva can now be seen. Marks on the cliff show that some of the houses had been three stories high. Some places on the cliff, which were apparently back-walls of rooms, were plastered and coated with white, and there are many pictographs on the rock. The masonry is of fair quality, but the stones were laid with more mortar than usual.

Figure 48 is a ground plan of a ruin which occurs at the point marked 46 on the map. It is situated in a cove in the rock at the top of

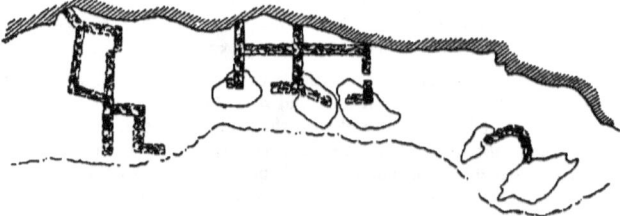

FIG. 48—Plan of cliff ruin No. 46.

the talus, 300 or 400 feet above the bottom, and immediately above the rectangular single room described and illustrated on page 151. It commands an extensive outlook over the bottom lands on both sides of the canyon and above. The cove is about 40 feet deep, and, though so high up, has been used as a sheep close, and doubtless some of the walls have been covered up. Four rooms are still standing in two little clusters of two rooms each. The walls of the rooms on the west are composed of large stones laid in plenty of mud mortar and plastered inside and out; those of the eastern portion were built of small stones, chinked but not plastered. One of the rooms is blackened by smoke in the corner only, as though there had been some chimney structure here, which subsequently had fallen away. The cliff walls back of the eastern part are heavily smoke-blackened; back of the western portion there are no stains. There is now no trace of a circular kiva, but there is a heavy deposit of sheep dung on the ground which might cover up such traces if they existed. This site commands one of the best outlooks in the canyon, but access, while not very difficult, is inconvenient on account of the great height above the bottom.

Figure 49 shows a common type of ruin in this class. The original structure appears to have contained one or two good rooms, which by subsequent additions have been divided into several. These later additions may have been made by the Navaho, who used the building material on the ground; at any rate the structure is now merely a cluster of storage cists.

One of the most extensive ruins of the cliff-outlook type situated in Canyon del Muerto is shown in figure 50. The plan shows at least eight

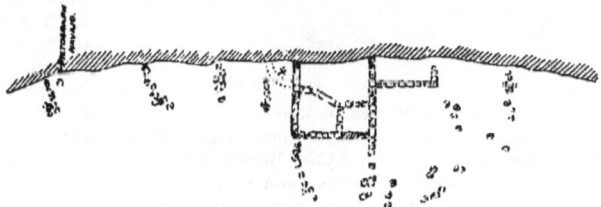

FIG. 49—Plan of cliff room with partitions.

rooms stretched along the cliff at the top of the talus. Figure 51 shows five rooms arranged in a cluster. One of these is still complete, the walls extending to the overhanging rock above which formed the roof. It will be noticed that the front room was set back far enough to allow access to the central room through a doorway in the corner. This was a convenience, rather than a necessity, for many of the rooms in ruins of this class were entered only through other rooms or through the roof, and a direct opening to the outer air was not considered a necessity;

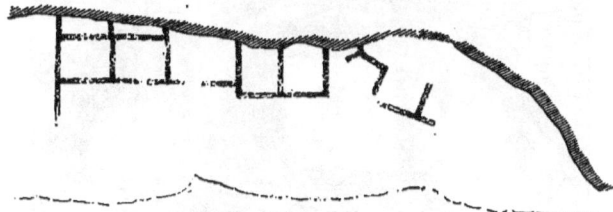

FIG. 50.—Plan of a large cliff outlook in Canyon del Muerto.

probably because these rooms in the cliff, which have been termed outlooks, were not in any sense watch towers, but rather places of abode during the harvest season, where the workers in the field lived when not actually employed in labor, and where the fields under cultivation could always be kept in view—an arrangement quite as necessary and quite as extensively practiced now as it was formerly.

Figure 52 shows a cluster of rooms in the little canyon called Tseonitsosi. This is another Casa Blanca, or White House, and, oddly enough,

16 ETH——10

it resembles its namesake in De Chelly, not only in the coat of whitewash applied to the front of the main room, but in having a subordinate

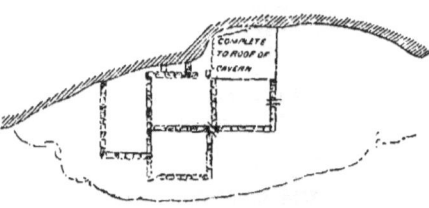

room to the left, over
which the wash ex-
tends, and in the
character of the site
it occupies. The
principal part of the
structure was built
in a cave, 18 or 20
feet from the ground,
across the front of
which walls extended

Fig. 51—Plan of a cluster of rooms in Canyon del Muerto.

as in the other Casa Blanca, and, like that ruin, there are also some
ruins at the foot of the cliff, on the flat. Figure 53 is a ground plan.
The resemblance to the other Casa Blanca, however, goes no further.
The ruin here illustrated represents a very small settlement, hardly
more than half a dozen rooms in all, and there is no trace of a circular
kiva, or other evidence of permanent habitation. It is possible that
the space between the edge of the floor of the cave above and the
whitened house back of it was occupied by some sort of structure, but
no evidence now remains which would warrant such a hypothesis, except
that the door of the white house is now about 4 feet above the ground.
The cave is only 40 feet long and a little over 10 feet deep, and there is
not room on the floor for more than three or four rooms, in addition to

Fig. 52—White House ruin in Tseonitsosi canyon.

those shown on the plan. The room on the right still preserves its roof
intact, showing the typical pueblo roof construction. It has a well-pre-
served doorway, and three other openings may be seen in the main room.

Apparently some effort at ornamentation was made here. The whitewash was not applied to the fronts of the two back rooms so as to cover

all of them, but in a broad belt, leaving the natural yellowish-gray color of the plastering in a narrow band above and a broad band below it. Moreover, the principal opening of the larger room was specially treated; in the application of the whitewash a narrow border or frame of the natural color was left surrounding it. The attempt to apply deco-

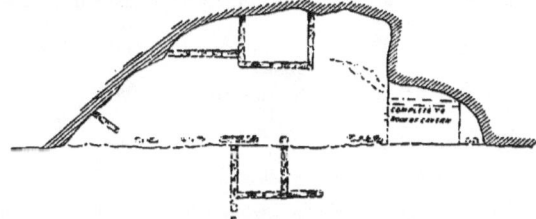

Fig. 53—Ground plan of a ruin in Tseonitsosi canyon.

ration not utilitarian in character is rare among the ruins here. It implies either a late period in the occupancy of this region, or an occupancy of the site by a people who had practiced this method of house-building longer or under more favorable conditions than the others.

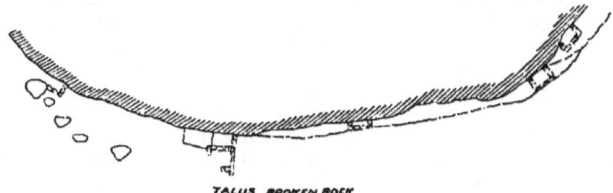

TALUS, BROKEN ROCK

Fig. 54—Plan of rooms against a convex cliff.

Figure 54 shows an arrangement of rooms along a narrow ledge at the top of the talus, where the cliff wall is not coved or concave, but convex. Some of these little rooms may have been used only for storage, but others were undoubtedly habitations. Figure 55 shows an

Fig. 55—Small ruin with curved wall.

example in which the back wall is curved, as though it was either built over an old kiva or an attempt was made to convert a rectangular room into a kiva. There were originally three rooms in the cluster, only one of which remains, but that one is of unusual size, measuring about 15 by 10 feet. If the room was used solely as a habitation, there was no necessity for the back wall, as the side walls continue back to the cliff. Including the little cove on the left, there are seven Navaho burial places on this site.

Plate LIII shows an outlook in the lower part of De Chelly, at the point marked 6 on the map. The lower part of the cliff here flares

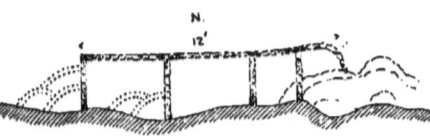

Fig. 56—Ground plan of a cliff outlook.

out slightly, forming a sharp slope; where it meets the vertical rock there is a small bench on which the ruin is situated. It is apparently inaccessible, but close examination shows a long series of hand and foot holes extending up a cleft in the rock, and forming an easy ascent. The site commands a good outlook over the bottom lands.

The ruin consists of three rectangular rooms arranged side by side against the cliff, and a kind of curved addition on the east. Figure 56 is a ground plan. The walls are still standing from a foot to 4 feet high, and produce the impression of being unfinished; although carefully chinked, they were neither plastered nor rubbed down. The two western rooms were built first, and the eastern wall extends through the front. East of these rooms there is a small rectangular chamber, and east of this again a low curved wall forming a little chamber or cist of irregular form (not shown in the plan). The front wall was extended beyond this and brought in again to the cliff on a curve, forming another small cist of irregular shape. This and the little chamber west of it were doubtless used for storage. They resemble in plan Navaho cists, but the masonry, which is exactly like the other walls here, will not permit the hypothesis of Navaho construction. Except for some slight traces in the northwest corner of the west room, there are no smoke stains about, nor are there any pictographs on the cliff walls. The western room was pierced by a window opening which was subsequently filled up, possibly by the Navaho, who have five burial cists here.

Fig. 57—Plan of cliff outlook No. 14, in Canyon de Chelly.

Figure 57 is the plan of a small outlook which occurs at the point marked 14 on the map. Opposite the mouth of Del Muerto there is an elevated rocky area of considerable extent, perhaps 50 feet above the bottom, but shelving off around the edges. Near the cliff this is covered by sand dunes and piles of broken rock; farther out there is a more level area covered thinly with sand and soil, and here there is a large ruin of the old obliterated type already described (page 93).

CLIFF OUTLOOK IN LOWER CANYON DE CHELLY

Near the edges the rock becomes bare again, and is 20 to 30 feet high, descending sheer or with an overhang to the bottoms or to the stream bed. On the western side, facing north, the ruin illustrated occurs. It is a mere cubby hole, and was evidently located for the area of cultivable land which lies before it, and which it almost completely commands. The cavity is about 12 feet above the ground and appears to have been divided by cross walls into three rooms, two of which were quite small. The back room was small, dark, and not large enough to contain a human body unless it was carefully packed in, and at various points along the back wall there are seeps of water. The interior of the little room was very wet and moldy at the time when it was examined, in winter, but in the summer time is probably dry enough.

FIG. 58—Ground plan of outlooks in a cleft.

The masonry is fair and the surface is finished with plaster. The open space in front of the small back room and the outer wall of the room itself are much blackened by smoke, as though the inhabitant lived here and used the small room only to store his utensils and implements. A small room on the east must have been used for a similar purpose. Both of these rooms were entered through narrow doorways opening on the principal space. The site is an ideal one for a lookout, but not well suited for a habitation. Plate LIV shows its character.

Cliff outlooks are often found on sites whose restricted areas preclude all possibility that they formed parts of larger settlements since obliterated. The ruin just described is an example. Another instance

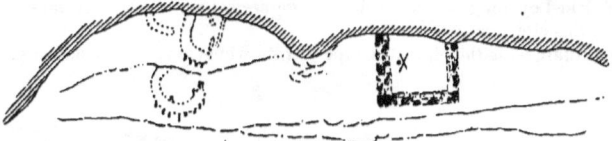

FIG. 59—Plan of a single-room outlook.

which occurs in Del Muerto is shown in figure 58. Here a deep cleft in the rock was partly occupied by two or three rooms. There was room for more, but apparently no more were built. There was not room, however, for even a small village. . There are several other examples in the canyon almost identical with these, but this type is not nearly so abundant as the succeeding. Figure 59 is a plan of a ruin near the mouth of Del Muerto. It was a single room, situated on a ledge perhaps 30 or 40 feet above the bottom land which it overlooked and of easy access.

FIG. 60—Three-room outlook in Canyon del Muerto.

This is the most common type of outlook or cliff ruin, and it might almost be said that they number hundreds, sometimes consisting of one room alone, sometimes of two or even three. The general appearance of these outlooks is shown in figure 60, which shows an example containing three rooms.

Figure 61 is a ground plan of an example containing two rooms, which occurs below the large ruin described before (No. 31, page 119), and figure 62 shows an example with one room, obscured and built over with Navaho cists. This site is located in the upper part of the canyon, on top of the talus, about 100 feet above the stream, and commands an outlook over several areas of bottom land on both sides. The walls are built about 10 feet high,

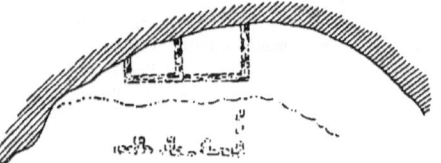

FIG. 61—Plan of a two-room outlook.

and are composed of medium-size stones laid in courses and carefully chinked with small spalls. The southwestern corner of the room is broken down, but the eastern wall is still standing, and shows a well-finished opening on that side. There are several Navaho burial cists on this site.

Figure 63 is the plan of a type of ruin which is rather anomalous in

FIG. 62—Plan of outlook and burial cists, No. 64.

the canyon. It occurs at the point marked 45 on the map, and occupies a small flat area almost on top of the talus 300 feet or more

CLIFF RUIN No. 14

above the stream bed. It is just below the ruin described and illustrated on page 144 (figure 48), and hardly 20 feet distant from it, and yet it does not appear to have been connected with it. It consists of a single large room, 20 feet long by 11½ feet wide outside, and the site commands an extensive prospect over bottom lands on both sides of the canyon, and above, but the only opening in the wall on that side is a little peephole 6 inches square and 2 feet from the ground. This is sufficient, however, to command nearly the whole outlook. There is a doorway on

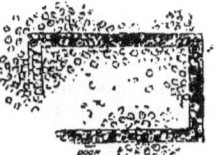

Fig. 63—Plan of rectangular room No. 45.

the eastern side, one side of which, fairly well finished, remains. There was apparently no other opening, unless one existed on the western side, where, in the center, the wall is broken down to within 2 feet of the ground. Along the western side of the room, at the present ground surface, there are remains of a bench about a foot wide; the eastern side is covered above this level.

The masonry is very rough and chinked only with large stones. The interior is roughly plastered in places, and small pieces of stone are stuck on flat. The corners are rounded. Externally the masonry has

Fig. 64—Rectangular single room.

the appearance of stones laid without mortar, like a Navaho stone corral, and were it not for the occurrence of other similar remains, it might be regarded as of Navaho or white man's construction, as the size,

site, plan, and masonry are all anomalous. Figure 64 shows an example,
however, closely resembling the one described in these features, and
figure 65 shows another. Altogether there are four or five examples,
distributed over a considerable area.

Somewhat similar wall remains are seen in places on the canyon
bottom, where they are always of modern Navaho origin, and it is
quite possible that the ruins above mentioned should be placed in the
same category. It will be noticed that in the plan the doorway or
entrance opening is on the eastern side—an invariable requirement of
Navaho house constructions; but it is only within recent times that the
Navaho have constructed permanent, rectangular abodes, and even
now such houses are rarely built. It is difficult to understand, moreover, why recourse should be had to such inconvenient sites, if the
structures are of Navaho origin, as these Indians always locate their
hogans on the bottom lands, or on some slight rise overlooking them.

Distributed throughout the canyons, wherever a favorable situation
could be found, there are a great number of sites resembling those of

Fig. 65—Single-room remains.

the cliff outlooks, but showing now no standing wall. There is always
some evidence of human occupancy, often many pictographs on the
back wall, as in an example in the lower part of the canyon shown in
plate LV. This occurs at point 2 on the map, in a cove perhaps 100
feet across, with caves on the northern and southern sides.

In the southern cave there are no traces of masonry, but the back of
the cave is covered with hand prints and pictographs of deer, as shown
in the plate. In the northern cave there are traces of walls. Many of
the sites do not show the faintest trace of house structures; some of
them have remains of storage cists, and many have remains of Navaho
burial cists, associated with pictographs not of Navaho origin. Some
idea of the number and distribution of these sites may be obtained from
the following list, wherein the numbers represent the location shown
on the detailed map: 2, 8, 9, 11, 18, 19, 21, 22, 23, 25, 26, 30, 38, 39, 40,
42, 43, 53, 54, 57, and 66—in all 21 sites which occur between the mouth

SITE MARKED BY PICTOGRAPHS

of De Chelly and the junction of Monument canyon, 13 miles above.
Beyond this point they are rare, as the areas of cultivable land become
scarce. A similar distribution prevails in Del Muerto.

DETAILS

SITES

The character of the site occupied by a ruin is a very important
feature where the response to the physical environment is as ready and
complete as it is in the ancient pueblo region. This feature has not
received the attention it deserves, for it is more than probable that in
the ultimate classification of ruins that will some day be formulated
the site occupied will be one of the principal elements considered, if
not the most important. The site is not so important per se, but must
be considered with reference to the specific character of the ruin upon
it, its ground plan, the character of other ruins in the vicinity which
may have been connected with it, and its topographic environment.
The character and ground plan of a cliff ruin would be so much out of
place on an open valley site that it would immediately attract attention.
The reverse is equally remarkable.

Considering all that has been written about the cliff ruins as defensive structures, it is strange how little direct evidence there is to support the hypothesis; how few examples can be cited which show
anything that can be construed as the result of the defensive motive
except the general impression produced on the observer. Nor, on the
other hand, do these ruins as a whole give any support to the theory
that they represent an intermediate stage in the development of the
pueblo people. Some few may, perhaps those examined by Mr F. H.
Cushing south and east of Zuñi do; but more than 99 per cent of them
give more support to a theory that they are the ultimate development
of pueblo architecture than to the other hypothesis, for they contain
in themselves evidence of a knowledge of construction equal and even
superior to that shown in many of the modern pueblo villages. The
only thing anomalous or distinctive about the cliff ruins, considered
as an element of pueblo architecture, is the character of site occupied.
If this were dictated by the defensive motive, it would seem reasonable
to suppose that the same motive would have some direct influence on
the structures, yet examples where it has affected the arrangement of
rooms or ground plan or the character of the masonry are exceedingly
rare and generally doubtful.

It is well to specify that in the preceding remarks the term cliff ruin
has been applied to small settlements, comprising generally less than
four rooms, sometimes only one or two, and usually located on high and
almost inaccessible sites. These are comprised in class IV of the classification here followed. Regular villages located in the cliffs or on top
of the talus (class III) are a different matter. These have nothing in
common with the small ruins, except that sometimes there is a similarity

of site. Doubtless in some of these ruins the defensive motive operated to a certain extent. In classes I and II, however, the influence of the defensive motive, in so far as it affected the character of site chosen, is conspicuous by its absence. As there is no evidence that the cliff ruins of class IV were separate and distinct from the other ruins, but the contrary, the defensive motive may be assigned a very subordinate place among the causes which produced that phase of pueblo architecture found in Canyon de Chelly.

An hypothesis as to the order in which sites of the various classes were occupied can not be based on the present condition of the ruins. It is more than likely that the older ruins served as quarries of building material for succeeding structures erected near them, and probably some of the cliff ruins themselves served in this way for the erection of others, for there are many sites from which the building stone has been almost entirely removed; yet there is no doubt that these sites were formerly occupied. The Navaho also have contributed to the destruction. Notwithstanding their horror of contact with the remains of the dead, quite a number of buildings have been erected by these Indians with material derived from adjacent ruins. It is evident that the gathering of this material would be a much lighter task than to quarry and prepare it, no matter how roughly the latter might be done.

In a study of some ruins in the valley of the Rio Verde, made a few years ago, a suggestion was made of the order in which ruins of various kinds succeeded one another—a sort of chronologic sequence, of which the beginning in time could not be determined. Studies of the ruins and inhabited villages of the old province of Tusayan (Moki) and Cibola (Zuñi), and a cursory examination of ruins on Gila river, show that they all fall easily into the same general order, which is somewhat as follows:

1. The earliest form of pueblo house is doubtful. As a rule, in most localities the earliest forms are already well advanced. As it is now known that the ancient pueblo region was not inhabited by a vast number of people, but by a comparatively small number of little bands, each in constant though slow movement, this condition is what we would expect to find. It is probable that the earliest settlements consisted of single houses or small clusters located in valleys convenient to areas of cultivable land and on streams or near water.

2. The next step gives us villages, generally of small size, located on the foothills of mesas and overlooking large areas of good land which were doubtless under cultivation. This class comprises more examples perhaps than any other, and many of them come well within the historic period, such as six of the seven villages of Tusayan at the time of the Spanish conquest in 1540, all of the Cibolan villages of the same date, and some of the Rio Grande pueblos of that time.

3. In some localities, though not in all, the small villages were at a later period moved to higher and more inaccessible sites. This change has taken place in Tusayan within the historic period, and in fact was

not wholly completed even fifty years ago. The pueblo of Acoma was in this stage at the time of the conquest, and has remained so to the present day. As a rule each of the small villages preserved its independence, but in some cases they combined together to occupy together a high defensive site. Such combination is, however, unusual.

4. The final stage in the development of pueblo architecture is the large, many-storied, or beehive village, located generally in the midst of broad valleys, depending on its size and population for defense, and usually adjacent to some stream. In this class of structure the defensive motive, in so far as it affected the choosing of the site, entirely disappears. The largest existing pueblo, Zuñi, made this step early in the eighteenth century; the next largest, Taos, was probably in this stage in 1540, and has remained so since. In some cases ruins on foothill sites (2) have merged directly into many-storied pueblos on open sites (4), without passing through an intermediate stage.

There is another step in the process of development which is now being taken by many pueblos, which, although an advance from the industrial point of view, is to the student of architecture degeneration. This consists of a return to single houses located in the valleys and on the bottom lands wherever convenience to the fields under cultivation required. This movement is hardly twenty years old, but is proceeding at a steadily accelerating pace, and its ultimate result is the complete destruction of pueblo architecture. Whatever we wish to know of this phase of Indian culture must be learned now, for two generations hence probably nothing will remain of it.

This hasty sketch will illustrate some of the difficulties that lie in the way of a complete classification of the ruins of the pueblo country. It is impossible to arrange them in chronologic sequence, because they are the product of different tribes who at different times came under the influence of analogous causes, and results were produced which are similar in themselves but different in time. It is believed, however, that the classification suggested exhibits a cultural sequence and probably within each tribe a chronologic order.

In this classification no mention has been made of the cliff and cave ruins. These structures belong partly to class III, villages on defensive sites, and partly to a subclass which pertained to a certain extent to all the others. In the early stages of pueblo architecture the people lived directly on the land they tilled. Later the villages were located on low foothills overlooking the land, but in this stage some of the villages had already attained considerable size and the lands overlooked by them were not sufficient for their needs. As a consequence some of the inhabitants had to work fields at a distance from the home village, and as a matter of convenience small temporary shelters were erected near by. In a still later stage, when the villages were removed to higher and more easily defended sites, the number of farming shelters must have largely increased, as suitable sites which also commanded large areas of good land could not often be found. At a still later stage, when the inhabitants of a number of small villages combined to form one large one, this difficulty was increased still more, and it is probable that in this stage the construction of outlying farming settlements attained its maximum development. Often whole villages of considerable size, sometimes many miles from the home pueblo, were nothing more than farming shelters. These villages, like the single-room shelters, were occupied only during the farming season; in the winter the inhabitants abandoned them completely and retired to the home village.

Some farming villages, such as those described above, are still in use among the pueblos. The little village of Moen-Kapi, attached to Oraibi, but 75 miles distant from it, is an example. There are also no fewer than three villages in the Zuñi country of the same class. Nutria, Pescado, and Ojo Caliente are summer villages of the Zuñi, although distant from that pueblo from 15 to 25 miles. It is significant that none of these subordinate villages possess a kiva. It is believed that the cliff ruins and cavate lodges, which are merely variants of each other due to geological conditions, were simply farming shelters of another type, produced by a certain topographic environment.

The importance which it is believed should attach to the site on which a ruin is found will be apparent from the above. It was certainly a prominent element in the De Chelly group. A study of the detailed map here published will illustrate how completely the necessity for proximity to an area of cultivable land has dominated the location of the settlements, large and small; and a visit to the place itself would show how little influence the defensive motive has exercised. Near the mouth of the canyon, where cultivable areas of land are not many, there are few ruins, but those which do occur overlook such lands. In the middle portion, where good lands are most abundant, ruins also are most abundant; while above this, as the rocky talus develops more and more, the ruins become fewer and fewer; and in the upper parts of the canyon, beyond the area shown on the map, they are located at wide distances apart, corresponding to little areas of good land so located. Not all of the available land was utilized, and only a small percentage of the available sites were built upon. Between the mouth of De Chelly and the junction of Monument canyon, 13 miles above, there are seventy-one ruins. A fair idea of their distribution may be obtained from a study of the detailed map (plate XLIII), in conjunction with the following figures:

I. Old villages on open sites occur at the points marked 12, 41, 52, 17a, 55, 60, 61, and 67; in all, nine sites; principally in the upper part of the canyon.

II. Home villages on bottom lands, located without reference to defense, occupy sites 3, 4, 17, 20, 28, 48, and 51; in all, seven sites. Probably there are many more ruins of this class and the preceding, now so far obliterated as to be overlooked or indistinguishable.

III. Home villages on defensive sites occur at the points marked 5, 10, 13, 15, 16, 27, 31, 32, 34, 36, 37, 40, 44, 47, 59, 62, and 66; in all, seventeen. This includes many sites where the settlements were very small, often only a few rooms, but there is always at least one kiva.

IV. Cliff outlooks and farming shelters occupy sites 2, 6, 7, 8, 9, 11, 14, 18, 19, 21, 22, 23, 24, 25, 26, 29, 30, 33, 35, 38, 39, 42, 43, 45, 46, 49, 50, 53, 54, 56, 57, 64, 63, 65, 68, 69, and 70; in all, thirty-seven, or more than half. Some of these sites are now marked only by Navaho remains, and possibly a small percentage of them are of Navaho making, but the sites which are clearly and unmistakably Navaho are not mentioned here. Of all the sites only one (No. 7) is actually inaccessible without artificial aid.

The absence of any attempt to improve the natural advantages of the sites is remarkable. No expedients were employed to make access either easier or more difficult, except that here and there series of hand and foot holes have been pecked in the rock. Steps, either constructed of masonry or cut in the rock, such as those found in the Mancos canyon and the Mesa Verde region, are never seen here. The cavities in which the ruins occur are always natural; they are never enlarged or curtailed or altered in the slightest degree, and very rarely is the cavity itself treated as a room, although there are some excellent sites for such treatment. The back wall of a cove is often the back wall of a village, but aside from this the natural advantages of the sites were seldom realized.

The settlements were always located with reference to the canyon bottom, and access was never had from above, notwithstanding that in some cases access from above was easier than from below. Yet the inhabitants must necessarily have obtained their supply of firewood from above, as the quantity in the canyons, especially in that part where most of the ruins occur, is very limited. The Navaho throw the wood over the cliffs, afterward gathering up the fragments below and carrying them on their backs to their hogans at various points on the canyon bottom. The crash of falling logs, dropped or pushed over the edge of a cliff, sometimes 400 or 500 feet high, is not an infrequent sound in the canyon, and is at first very puzzling to the visitor.

The canyon walls are so nearly vertical, or rather so large a proportion is vertical, that egress or ingress, except at the mouth of the canyon, is a matter of great difficulty. Near the junction of Monument canyon, 13 miles above the mouth of De Chelly, there is a practicable horse trail ascending a narrow gorge to the southeast. The Navaho call it the Bat trail, on account of its difficulties. Another horse trail crosses Del Muerto some 8 or 10 miles above its mouth. With these exceptions there is no point where a horse can get into the canyons or out of them, but there are dozens of places where an active man, accustomed to it, can scale the walls by the aid of foot-holes which have been pecked in the rock at the most difficult places. These foot trails are in constant use by the Navaho, who ascend and descend by them with apparent ease, but it is doubtful whether a white man could be induced to climb them, except perhaps under the stress of necessity. There are even some trails over which sheep and goats are driven in and out of the canyon, but anyone who had not seen the flocks actually passing over the rocks would declare such a feat impossible. Some of these trails at least are of Navaho origin. Whether any of them were used by the former dwellers in the canyon can not now be determined; it seems probable that some of them were.

Plate LVI shows a characteristic site in the lower part of the canyon. It occurs at the point marked 8 on the map, and is now quite

FIG. 66—Site apparently very difficult of access.

difficult of approach, owing to the wearing away or weathering of a long line of foot-holes in the sloping rock, but formerly access was easy enough. It is now marked by a cluster of Navaho burial cists. Figure 66 shows an example that occurs in De Chelly, about 8 miles

SITE DIFFICULT OF APPROACH

above the junction of Monument canyon. At first glance, and at a distance, this site appears to be really inaccessible, but a close inspection of the figure will show that it could be reached with comparative little difficulty over the rounded mass of rock shown to the left. By cutting off that side of the figure it could be made to serve as an illustration of a wholly inaccessible ruin.

MASONRY

The ancient pueblo builder, like his modern successor, was so closely in touch with nature, so dependent on his immediate physical surroundings, that variations in some at least of his arts are more natural and to be expected than uniformity. Especially is this true of the art of construction, and variations in masonry are more often than not the result of variations in the material employed, which is nearly always that most convenient to hand. Yet there were other conditions that necessarily influenced it, such, for example, as the character of the structure to be erected, whether permanent or temporary. The summer village of Ojo Caliente presents a type of masonry much ruder than any found in the home village of Zuñi, although both were built and occupied by the same people at the same time.

Within the limits of Canyon de Chelly, where the physical conditions and the character of material are essentially uniform, a considerable variation in the masonry is found, implying that some conditions other than the usual ones have influenced it. Were the masonry of one class of ruins inferior or superior throughout to that of another it might be easily explained, but variations within each class are greater than those between classes. Conditions analogous to those which prevailed in the case of Ojo Caliente and Zuñi may have governed here, or there may have been other conditions of which we now know nothing. It may be that sites originally occupied as farming shelters subsequently became regular villages, as has happened in other regions. The position of the kivas in many of the ruins suggests this. As a whole the masonry is inferior to that found in the Mancos canyon and the Chaco, and superior to that of Tusayan, but, as in Tusayan, where the masonry is sometimes very roughly constructed, the builders were well acquainted with the methods which produced the finer and better work.

The highest type of masonry in the pueblo system of architecture consists of small blocks of stone of nearly uniform size, dressed, and laid in courses, and rubbed down in situ. No attempt was made to break joints. This system requires the careful preparation of the material beforehand, and examples of it are not very common in Canyon de Chelly. As a variant we have walls composed of stones of fairly uniform size, laid with the best face out and with the interstices chinked with small spalls. The chinking is carried to such an extent in some places, as in the Chaco ruins, that the walls present the effect of a mosaic composed of small spalls. Chinking is almost a universal practice, and in some localities had passed, or was passing, from a mere constructive to a real decorative feature. Here we have the beginning of that architecture which has been defined by Fergnson as "ornamental and ornamented construction"—in other words, of architecture as an art rather than as a craft.

The use of an exterior finish of plaster was conducive to poor masonry. Such plastering is found throughout the region, but it is much more abundant in the modern than in the ancient work. Perhaps we may find in this a suggestion of relative age; not in the use of plastering, but in its prevalence.

Pueblo masonry is composed of very small units, and the results obtained testify to the patience and industry of the builders rather than to their knowledge and skill. In fact, their knowledge of construction was far more limited than would at first sight be supposed. The marked tabular character of the stone used rendered but a small amount of preparation necessary for even the best masonry. For over 90 per cent of it there was no preparation other than the selection of material. The walls and buildings were always modified to suit the ground, never the reverse, and instances in which the site was prepared are very rare, if not indeed unknown. There are no such instances in De Chelly, where sites were often irregular, and a small amount of work would have rendered them much more desirable.

Plate LVII shows a type of masonry which is quite common in De Chelly. It is the west room of ruin 16, near the mouth of Del Muerto An attempt at regularity, and possibly at decorative effect, is apparent in the use of courses of fairly uniform thickness, alternating with other courses or belts composed of small thin fragments. Beautiful examples of masonry constructed on this method occur in the Chaco ruins, but here, while the method was known, the execution was careless or faulty. Chinking with small spalls has been extensively practiced and gives the wall an appearance of smoothness and finish. A similar wall, rather better constructed, occurs at the point marked 3 on the map, and in this case the stones composing the wall were rubbed down in situ. Another wall, which occurs in the same ruin, is shown in plate LVIII. In places very large stones have been used, larger than one man could handle conveniently, but the general effect of the wall face is very good. This effect was obtained by placing the best face of the stone outward and by careful chinking.

Chinking was sometimes done, not with slips of stone driven in with a hammer, after the usual style, but with bits of mud pressed in with the fingers. The mud was used when about the consistency of modeling clay, and bears the imprints of the fingers that applied it; even the skin markings show clearly and distinctly. From this use of mud to its use as an exterior plaster there is but a short step; in fact, examples which are intermediate can be seen throughout the canyon. In places mud has been applied to small cracks and cavities in larger quantities than was necessary, and the excess has been smoothed over the

MASONRY IN CANYON DE CHELLY

adjacent stones forming a wall partly plastered, or plastered in patches. Plate LIX, which shows the interior of a room in ruin 10, will illustrate this. Here the process has been carried so far that the wall is almost plastered, but not quite. In plastered walls the process was carried a step farther, and the surface was finished by the application of a final coat of mud made quite liquid. The interior plastering of kivas was always much more carefully done than that of any other walls. Owing to blackening by smoke and recoating, the thickness of the plastering in kivas can be easily made out. Often it is as thin as ordinary paper.

Plate LX shows walls in which an abundance of mud mortar was used, and the effect is that of a plastered wall. The difference between these walls and those shown in plate LVII is only one of degree, the wall shown in plate LIX being of an intermediate type. No instance occurs in the canyon where a coating of mud was evenly applied to the whole surface of a wall, in the way, for example, that stucco is used by us. It seems probable, therefore, that the application of plaster as a finish grew out of the use of stone spalls for chinking, and its prevalence in modern as compared with old structures is suggestive. It is not claimed, however, that because we have examples of the intermediate stages in De Chelly that the process was developed there. The step is such a slight one that it might have been made in a hundred different localities at a hundred different times or at one time; but it is well to note that in any given group of ruins or locality it is likely to be later than masonry chinked with stones. Surface finishing in mud plaster is the prevailing method at the present day, and well-executed masonry of stone carefully chinked is almost invariably ancient. The use of surface plaster is largely responsible for the deterioration of stonework that has taken place since the beginning of the historic period. The modern village of Zuñi, which dates from the beginning of the eighteenth century, although built on the site of an older village, is essentially a stone-built village, though that fact would never appear from a cursory examination, so completely is the stonework covered by surface plaster.

In Tusayan (Moki) walls have been observed in progress of erection. The stones were laid up dry, and some time after, when the rains came and pools of water stood here and there in pockets on the mesa top, mud mortar was mixed and the interstices were filled. This method saved the transportation of water from the wells below up to the top of the mesa, a task entailing much labor. Doubtless a similar method was followed in De Chelly, where the stream bed carries water only during a part of the year. But stone was also actually laid in mud mortar, as shown in plate LII, which illustrates a rough type of masonry.

It is probable that the practice of chinking grew up out of the scarcity of water, when walls were erected during the dry season and finished when the rains made the manufacture of mud mortar less of a task. The rough wall shown in the illustration is the outside of an interior wall of a kiva, and it was probably covered by the rectangular

16 ETH——11

inclosing wall that came outside of it. It will be noticed that chinking, both with mud and with spalls, was extensively practiced and seems here to have been an essential part of the construction. In this example it could have no relation to the finish of the wall, for the wall was not finished.

Much of the masonry in the canyon is of the type described, but examples differ widely in degree of finish and in material selected. Some of the walls appear very rough and even crude, so much so that they almost appear to be the first efforts of a people at an unknown art, but a closer inspection shows that even the rudest walls were erected with a knowledge of the principles which were followed in the best ones, and that the difference resulted only from the care or lack of care employed. The rudest walls are much superior to the masonry of the Navaho cists which are found in conjunction with them and which are constructed on a different method.

Although walls were often built on sloping rock, and the builders had experience and at times disastrous experience to guide them, the necessity for a flat and solid foundation was never appreciated. Walls were sometimes built on loose débris; even refuse which had been covered and formed an artificial soil was considered sufficient. There are many instances in the canyon where lack of foresight or lack of knowledge in this respect has brought about the destruction of walls. Walls resting on foreign material occur throughout the region; they are not confined to any one class of ruins or to any part of the canyon, but are found as much or more in the most recent as in the most ancient examples. Mummy Cave ruin and Casa Blanca are good examples. In the latter the small room on the left of the upper group (plate XLVII) is especially interesting. The side walls appear to rest on a deposit of refuse nearly 2 feet thick, which in turn rests on the sloping rock. The front wall is supported by a buttress as shown; without this support it would certainly have been pushed out. The buttress appears to have been built at the same time as the front wall, although its use in this way is not aboriginal. The whole arrangement is such as would result if this room, originally represented by a low front wall perhaps, were constructed when the site became inadequate and consequently at a late period in its occupancy.

The character of the refuse and débris upon which some of the walls rest is worth notice. It is well known that sheep were introduced into this country by the Spaniards, and the presence in the ruins of sheep dung, or of a material which closely resembles it, is important. Much of this is due to subsequent Navaho occupancy, and many ruins are used today by these Indians as sheepfolds. It is said, moreover, that at the time of the Navaho war, when the soldiers bayoneted all the sheep they could find, large flocks were driven up into some cliff ruins that are almost inaccessible, and kept there for a time in security. But many instances are found where the walls rest directly upon layers

CHINKED WALLS IN CANYON DE CHELLY

of compacted dung. An example is shown in plate LII, and others are mentioned in the text under the descriptions of various ruins.

It has been suggested that the compacted dung found in the ruins was the product not of sheep, but of some other domesticated animal which existed in this country at the time of the first Spanish invasion, but the evidence to support this hypothesis is so very slight that so far the suggestion is only a suggestion. Not the slightest trace of this animal has been found, although it is alleged that it was domesticated among the pueblos three hundred and fifty years ago.

Although the idea of a strengthening or supporting buttress is thought to be a foreign introduction, a hypothesis that is strengthened by the occurrence of other features, the masonry itself is aboriginal in its principles and probably also in execution. The conservatism of the Indian mind in such matters is well known. The Zuñi today use stone more than adobe, although for a hundred years or more there has been an adobe church in the midst of the village.

Adobe construction in this region is only partially successful. North of the Gila river, in the plateau country, the climate is not suited to it; the rains are too heavy and the frosts are destructive. Constant vigilance and prompt repairs are necessary, and even then the adobe work is not satisfactory. Certainly in the northern part of the country the aborigines would not have developed this method of construction in the face of the difficulties with which it is surrounded; yet there are examples of adobe work in some of the most important ruins in De Chelly, as has already been stated. The fact that the only previously known examples of adobe work occur in ruins which are known to have been inhabited subsequent to the Spanish conquest, such as the ruin of Awatobi, in Tusayan, is suggestive. Moreover, adobe construction in this region belongs to a late period; for the walls are almost always very thin, usually 6 or 7 inches. The old type of massive walls, 2 or even 3 feet thick, are seldom or never found constructed of adobe, although such thickness is more necessary in this material than in stone.

There is another method of construction which, although not masonry, should be noticed here. This is the equivalent of the Mexican "jacal" construction, and consists of series of poles or logs planted vertically in the ground close to each other and plastered with mud either outside or on both sides. The only example of this found in the canyon occurs in the western part of the lower Casa Blanca ruin, and has already been mentioned. Did it not occur elsewhere it could be dismissed here as simply another item of evidence of the modern occupancy of the ruin, but Dr W. R. Birdsall mentions walls in the Mesa Verde ruins which are "continued upward upon a few tiers of stone by wickerwork heavily plastered inside and outside"[1] and Nordenskiöld mentions a similar construction in the interior of a kiva. Whether a similar foundation or lower part of stone existed in the Casa Blanca ruin could not be determined without excavation.

---

[1] Bull. Am. Geog. Soc., vol. XXIII, p. 598.

OPENINGS

The ruins in De Chelly are so much broken down that few examples of openings now remain; still fewer are yet intact; but there is no doubt that they are of the regular pueblo types. Most of the openings in the De Chelly ruins are rectangular, of medium size, neither very large nor very small, with unfinished jambs and sills, and with a lintel such as that shown in plate LVIII, composed of one or two series of light sticks, sometimes surmounted by a flat stone slab. This example occurs at the point marked 3 on the map, in what was formerly an extensive village. The wall on the left, now covered by loosely piled rocks, was pierced by a narrow notched doorway. The opening shown in the illustration, which is in the northern wall, is 2 feet high and 14 inches wide; its sill is about 18 inches from the ground. The lintel is composed of six small sticks, about an inch in diameter, surmounted by a flat slab of stone, very roughly shaped, and separated from the sticks by 2 inches of mud mortar.

Plate LVII shows an opening which occurs in ruin No. 16. The

FIG. 67—Notched doorway in Canyon de Chelly.

building consisted of two rooms, between which there was no communication. The eastern room was entered by the doorway shown in the illustration, which is 2 feet above the ground and 2 feet high. To facilitate ingress a notch was dug in the wall about 8 inches from the ground. The western room was entered through a large doorway, shown in plate LI. The sill is about 8 inches above the ground; the opening is 3 feet high and 14 inches wide. The lintel is composed of small sticks, with a slab of stone above them, and the top of the opening and perhaps the sides were plastered.

The notched or T-shape doorway, which is quite common in the Mesa Verde ruins and in Tusayan, is not abundant in De Chelly, but some examples can be seen there. One is shown in figure 67, which illustrates the type. There is no doubt that doorways of this kind developed at a time when no means existed for closing the opening, except blankets or skins, and when loads were carried on the backs of men. It often happened that doorways originally constructed of this style were afterward changed by partial filling to square or rectangular openings. The principal doorway in the front wall of the White House proper was originally of T-shape; at some later period, but before

A PARTLY PLASTERED WALL

the white coating was applied, the left-hand wing and the standard below it were filled in, leaving an almost square opening. This later filling is not uncommon in De Chelly, and is often found in Tusayan, where openings are sometimes reduced for the winter season and enlarged again in the summer. Many openings are completely closed, either by filling in with masonry or by a stone slab, and examples of both of these methods are found in De Chelly. In the third wall from the east, in the upper part of Casa Blanca ruin, there is a well-finished doorway sealed by a thin slab of stone set in mud. On the right side of the opening, about the middle, a loop or staple of wood has been built into the wall, and in the corresponding place on the left side a stick about half an inch in diameter projects. An opening into the small room west of the White House proper has a similar contrivance, and another example occurs in the front wall of the small single room in the eastern end of the ruin. Oddly enough the three examples that occur in this ruin are all found in adobe walls.

This feature appears to have been a contrivance for temporarily closing openings which were provided with stone slabs, and the latter were sealed in place with mud mortar when it was desired to close the room permanently. Examples, identical even in details, have been found in the Mancos canyon, and one is described and illustrated by Chapin,[1] who states that the slab was 14½ inches wide at one end, 15½ at the other, and 25 inches high, with an average thickness of an inch. He mentions staples on both sides. Nordenskiöld[2] illustrates another or possibly the same example. He notes, however, an inner frame composed of small sticks and mud against which the slab rested. He thinks the notched doorways belonged to rooms most frequented in daily life, while the others belonged in general to storerooms or other chambers requiring a door to close them.

Taken as a whole, the settlements in De Chelly appear to have been well provided with doorways and other openings, and there is no perceptible difference in this respect between the various classes of ruins. Openings were freely left in the walls, wherever convenience dictated, and without regard to the defensive motive, which, in the large valley pueblos, brought about the requirement that all the first-story rooms should be entered from the roof, a requirement which has only recently given way to the greater convenience of an entrance on the ground level.

ROOFS, FLOORS, AND TIMBER WORK

In the pueblo system of construction roofs and floors are the same; in other words, the roof of one room is the floor of the room above, and where a room or house is but one story high no change in the method of construction is made. The erection of walls was only a question of time, as the unit of the masonry is small; but the construction of a roof was a much harder task, as the beams were necessarily

[1] Land of the Cliff Dwellers. pp. 149–150, pl. opp. p. 155.
[2] Cliff Dwellers of the Mesa Verde. pp. 52–53, fig. 28.

brought from a distance, sometimes a very long distance. The Tusayan claim that some of the timbers used in the construction of the
mission buildings, which were established prior to the insurrection of
1680, were brought on the backs of men from San Francisco mountains, a distance of over 100 miles, and references to the transportation
of timber over long distances are not uncommon in Pueblo traditions.
In De Chelly great difficulty must have been experienced in procuring
an adequate supply, as in that portion of the canyon where most of the
ruins occur no suitable trees grow. Doubtless in many cases, where
the location under overhanging cliffs permitted, roofs were dispensed
with, but this alone would not account for the dearth of timber found
in the ruins. If we suppose the canyon to have been the scene of a
number of occupancies instead of one, the absence of timber work, as
well as the much obliterated appearance of some of the ruins, would
be explained, for the material would be used more than once, perhaps
several times. The Navaho would not use the timber in cliff ruins
under any circumstances, and they would rather starve than eat food
cooked with it. Many of the cliff outlooks, being occupied only during
the farming season and being also fairly well sheltered, were probably
roofless.

Timber was used as an aid to masonry construction in two ways—as
a foundation and as a tie. Many instances can be seen where the walls
rest on beams, running, not with them, but across them. These beams
were placed directly on the rock, and the front walls rested partly on
their ends and partly on the rock itself. Plate LII shows the end of
one of these beams. In nine cases out of ten the beams do not appear
to have served any useful end, but perhaps if the walls were removed
down to the foundations the purpose would be clear. Sometimes a
beam was placed on the rock in the line of the wall above it. The
single or separate room occupying the western end of the upper cave
in the Casa Blanca ruin is an example of this use. The front wall rests
on beams, as shown in plate XLVI. Some of the back adobe walls in
the eastern part of the upper ruin rest on timbers, and instances of this
feature are not uncommon in other parts of the canyon. The southeastern corner of the tower in Mummy Cave ruin in Del Muerto rested
on timbers apparently laid over a small cavity or hole in the rock. The
timber was not strong enough to support the weight placed upon it, and
consequently gave way, letting the corner of the tower fall out.

Cross walls were sometimes tied to front or back walls by timbers
built into them, but this method, of which fine examples can be seen in
the Chaco ruins, was but slightly practiced here. Timber was used
also to prevent the slipping of walls on sloping sites, being placed vertically and built into the masonry; but as this use is a constructive
expedient it is discussed under that head.

STORAGE AND BURIAL CISTS

Facilities for the storage of grain and other produce are essential
in the pueblo system of horticulture, as in any other. As a result,
storage cists are found everywhere. In the modern pueblos the inner

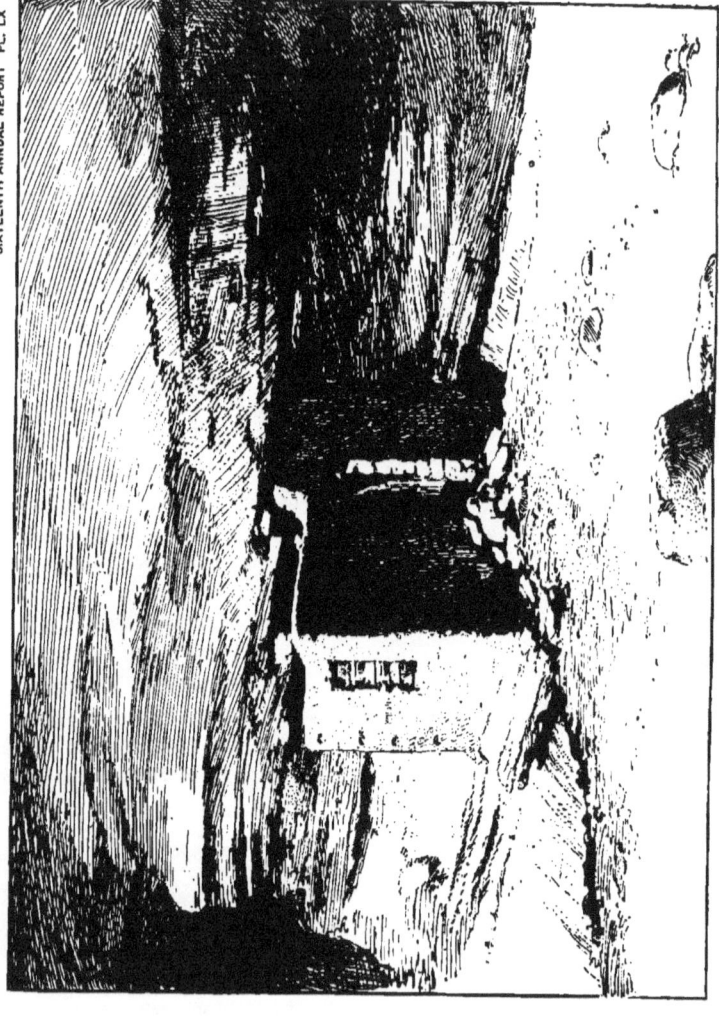

PLASTERED WALL IN CANYON DE CHELLY

dark rooms, which would otherwise be useless, provide the necessary space, but in the settlements in De Chelly, which were very small as a rule, there were few such rooms, and special structures had to be erected. These differed from the dwelling rooms only in size, although as a rule, perhaps, the openings by which they were entered were not so large as those of the dwellings and were sometimes, possibly always, provided with some means by which they could be closed.

Immense numbers of these storage cists are found in the canyon, some of them with masonry so roughly executed that it is difficult to discriminate between the old pueblo and the modern Navaho work. Sometimes these cists or small rooms form part of a village, more often they are attached to the cliff outlooks, and not infrequently they stand alone on sites overlooking the lands whose product they contained. It is probable that many of the cliff outlooks themselves were used quite as much for temporary storage as for habitations during the farming season. These two uses, although quite distinct, do not conflict with each other. Doubtless many excellent sites, now marked only by the remains of storage cists, were occupied also during the summer as outlooks without the erection of any house structures. Some of the modern pueblos now use temporary shelters of brush for outlooks.

It is not meant that the crops when gathered were placed in these cists and kept there until used. The harvest was, as a rule, permanently stored in the home villages, and the cists were used only for temporary storage. Doubtless the old practice resembled somewhat that followed by the Navaho today. The harvest is gathered at the proper time and what is not eaten at once is hidden away in cists of old or modern construction. If it is well hidden, the grain may remain in the cists for a long time if not withdrawn for consumption; but as a rule it is taken away a few months later. The annual emigration of the Navaho commences soon after the harvest, and at intervals during the winter and spring, and in summer, if the supply is not then exhausted, visits are paid to the cists and portions of the grain are carried away.

A large proportion of the cists are of modern Navaho work, but that some of them were used by the pueblo people who preceded them seems probable from the similarity in horticultural methods, and from the small size of many of the villages. A village inhabited by half a dozen people was not uncommon; one which could accommodate more than fifty was rare. Moreover, some of the storage cists that occur in conjunction with dwellings differ from the latter only in size and in their separation from the other rooms. The masonry is quite as good as that of the houses, and much superior to the Navaho work. .

Plate LXI shows an example which occurs in the lower part of the canyon, at the point marked 1 on the map. It is placed on a little ledge or block of rock, 12 feet above the stream and about 8 feet above the bottom land below it. This is the first considerable area of bottom land in the canyon. The cist is 2 feet square inside and occupies the whole width of the rock. An exceptionally large amount of mud plaster was used on the walls, which are better finished outside than inside. Access was had by hand-holes in the rock, now almost obliterated. Originally the structure consisted of two or more rooms.

A little below this site there are some well-executed pictographs, and on some rocks immediately to the right some crude work of the Navaho of the same sort. To the left of the cist a round hole 6 or 8 inches in diameter has been pecked into the almost vertical face of the rock. The purpose of this is not clear.

The storage of water was so seldom attempted, or perhaps so seldom necessary, that only one example of a reservoir was found. This has already been described (page 126). If the cliff ruins were defensive structures, a supply of water must have been kept in them, and where this requirement was common, as it would be under the hypothesis, certainly some receptacle other than jars of pottery would be provided. Few, if any, of the cliff outlooks are so situated that a supply of water could be procured without descending to the stream bed, and without a supply of water the most impregnable site in the canyon would have little value.

The number of burial cists in the canyon is remarkable; there are hundreds of them. Practically every ruin whose walls are still standing contains one or more, some have eight or ten. They are all of Navaho origin and in many of them the remains of Navaho dead may still be seen. Possibly the Navaho taboo of their own dead has brought about the partial taboo of the cliff dwellers' remains which prevails, and which is an element that must be taken into account in any discussion of the antiquity of the ruins.

The burial cists are built usually in a corner or against a wall of a cliff dweller's house, but sometimes they are built against a cliff wall, and occasionally stand out alone. The masonry is always rough, much inferior to the old walls against which it generally rests, and usually very flimsy. The structures are dome-shape when standing alone, or in the shape of a section of a dome when placed against other walls. The natural bedding of the stone is sometimes wholly ignored, and in some cases the walls consist merely of thin slabs of stone on edge, held together with masses of mud, the whole presenting an average thickness of less than 3 inches. Such structures on ordinary sites would not last six months; protected as they are they might last for many years.

Not all the Navaho dead in the canyon find their last resting place in the ruins. Graves can be seen under bowlders and rocks high up on the talus; and in one place in De Chelly a number of little piles of stones are pointed out as the burial places of "many Americans," who, it is said, were killed by the Navaho in their last war. It is also said that in the olden days, when the Navaho considered De Chelly their stronghold and the heart of their country, the remains of prominent

STORAGE CIST IN CANYON DE CHELLY

men of the tribe were often brought to the canyon for interment in the
ruins. Such burials are still made, both in the ruins themselves and in
cists on similar sites.

As a whole the Navaho burial cists are much more difficult of access
than the ruins, and some of them appear to be now really inaccessible,
a statement which can be made of but few ruins. Some of them appear
to have been reached from above. The agility and dexterity of the
Navaho in climbing the cliffs is remarkable, and possibly some of the
sites now apparently inaccessible are not so considered by them. As
before stated, there are a number of Navaho foot trails out of the canyon, where shallow pits or holes have been pecked in the rock as an
aid in the more difficult places, and similar aids were often employed
to afford access to storage and burial cists. Plate LVI shows a

FIG. 68—Cist composed of upright slabs.

site in the lower part of the canyon where such means have been
employed. The pits in the rock are so much worn by atmospheric erosion that the ascent now is very dangerous. The cove or ledge to which
they lead is about halfway up the cliff, and on it are a number of cists,
one of them still intact, with a doorway. The masonry consists of large
slabs of sandstone set on edge, sometimes irregularly one above another,
the whole being roughly plastered inside and out. About 200 yards
farther up the cove, on the same side, there is a series of foot holes
leading to a small cave about halfway up, and thence upward and
probably out of the canyon. They are probably of Navaho origin.

The use of stone on edge is apparently confined to these cists. Figure
68 shows a structure which occurs a little above the ruin marked 37
on the map. The walls consist of thin slabs of stone set upright and

roughly plastered where they meet. Instances of the use of stone in this way are not uncommon in the pueblo country, and there are a number of examples in De Chelly.

As before stated, the typical Navaho burial cist is of dome shape. The roof or upper portion is supported on sticks so arranged as to leave a small square opening in the top. Apparently at some stage in its existence this hole is closed and sealed, but examples were examined which were very old and one which was but twenty-four hours old, but in neither case was the opening closed. Doubtless the opening has some ceremonial significance; it is not of any actual use, as it is too small to permit the passage of a human body. Plate LXII shows a typical cist in good order and another such broken down. These examples occur at the point marked 6 on the map, in the ruin shown in plate LIII. This site is of comparatively easy access, and there are many others equally easy or even more so, but, on the other hand, there are many sites which now seem to be wholly inaccessible.

DEFENSIVE AND CONSTRUCTIVE EXPEDIENTS

The cliff ruins have always been regarded as defensive structures, sometimes even as fortresses, but in De Chelly whatever value they have in this respect is due solely to the sites they occupy. There are many places here where slight defensive works on the approaches to sites would increase their value a hundredfold, but such works were apparently never constructed. Furthermore, the ruins themselves never show even a suggestion of the influence of the defensive motive, except in the two possible instances already mentioned. The ordinary or dwelling-house plan has not been at all modified, not even to the extent that it has in the modern pueblos. If the cliff ruins were defensive structures it would certainly seem that an influence strong enough to bring about the occupancy of such inconvenient and unsuitable sites would also be strong enough to bring about some modifications in the architecture, modifications which would render more suitable sites available. The influence of the physical environment on pueblo architecture, and the sensitiveness of the latter to such influence, has already been commented on. Moreover, it also has been stated that, so far as known, but one instance occurs in the canyon where provision was made for the storage of water; yet without water the strongest "fortress" in the canyon could not withstand a siege of forty-eight hours. Further, assuming that the structures were defensive, and well prepared to resist attack, if necessary, for several days, only a few such attacks would be required to cause their abandonment, for the crops on the canyon bottom, practically the sole possessions of the dwellers in the canyon, would necessarily be lost.

These are some of the difficulties that stand in the way of the assumption that the cliff ruins were defensive structures or permanent homes. If, however, we adopt the hypothesis that they were farming outlooks

NAVAHO BURIAL CISTS

occupied only during the farming season, and then only for a few days or weeks at a time, after the manner that such outlooks are used by the Pueblo Indians at the present time, most of the difficulties vanish.

The apparent inaccessibility of many of the sites disappears on close examination, and we must not forget that places really difficult of access to us would not necessarily be so regarded by a people accustomed to that manner of life. Many locations which could not be surpassed as defensive sites were not occupied, while others much inferior in this respect were built upon. It was very seldom that the natural conditions were modified, even to the extent of selecting a route of access other than that which would naturally be followed, and, of course, the easiest route for the cliff dwellers would be also the easiest route for their enemies. In many cases the easiest way of access, which was the one used by the cliff dwellers, was not direct. It was not commanded by the immediate site of the dwellings, except in its upper part, and in some cases not at all. Enemies could climb to the very doors of the houses before they could be seen or attacked. The absence of military knowledge and skill, and of any attempt to fortify or strengthen a site, or even to fully utilize its natural defensive advantages, is characteristic of the cliff ruins of De Chelly. If the cliff dwellers were driven to the use of such places by a necessity for defense, this absence is remarkable, especially as there is evidence that the settlements were occupied for a number of, perhaps a great many, years.

Under the head of constructive expedients we have a different result. The difficulties which came from the occupancy of exceptional sites were promptly reflected in the construction, and unusual ways and methods were adopted to overcome them. These methods are the more interesting in that they were not always successful. It sometimes happened that walls had to be placed on a foundation of smooth, sloping rock. In such cases the rock was never cut away, but timbers were employed to hold the wall in place. In some instances the timbers were laid at right angles to the line of front wall, at points where cross walls joined it inside. The front wall thus rested partly on the ends of timbers and partly on rock, while the other ends of the timbers were held in place by the cross walls built upon them. An example of this construction is shown in plate LII. In other instances, where the surface was irregular but did not slope much, timbers were laid on the wall lines and the masonry rested partly upon them. An example of this occurs in the Casa Blanca ruin, shown in plate XLVII. Still another method of using timber in masonry occurs in a number of ruins. It was seldom effective and apparently was confined to this region. This consists of the incorporation into the masonry of upright logs. Figure 69 shows an example that occurs at the point marked 32 on the map. The site here is an especially difficult one, as the builders were compelled to place walls not only on sloping rock foundations, but also on loose débris, and the vertical timber support is quite common.

The three kivas which are shown on the plan occupied the front of the village, and their front walls have fallen out. Apparently the same accident has happened at least once, if not several times, before, and a fragment of a previous front wall has slipped down 3 or 4 feet, and was left there when the kiva was repaired. The round dots shown on the plan, two in the wall of the central kiva and one on the east, represent vertical timbers incorporated in the masonry. The tops of these logs reach the level of the top of the bench in the kiva, and their lower ends rest in cavities in the rocks. The eastern one was removed and was found to be about 2 feet long. The upper half was charred, although formerly inclosed completely in the masonry, as though it had been burned off to the required length. The lower end was hacked off with some blunt implement, and as nearly squared as it could be done with such means. It was set into a socket or hole pecked in the solid rock

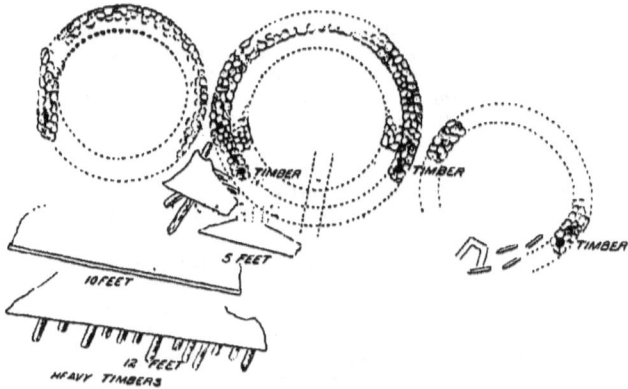

FIG. 69—Retaining walls in Canyon de Chelly.

and plastered in with clay. In the outer portion of the eastern wall of the central kiva there are many marks of sticks, 3 to 4 inches in diameter and placed vertically.

Although timbers as an aid to masonry occur in many ruins, they predominate in those which have been suggested as the sites most recently occupied; but in the Chaco ruins timber has been used extensively and much more skillfully than here. Instances occur where a cross wall has been tied into a front wall with timber, and so effective was the device that in one instance a considerable section of cross wall can be seen suspended in the air, being completely broken out below and now supported wholly by the ties. Instances can also be seen where partition walls are supported on crossbeams at some distance from the ground, forming large and convenient openings between rooms; but nothing of that kind was seen in De Chelly. In the latter region

wherever horizontal timbers are used for the support of masonry they rest on the bed rock.

The same ruin (No. 32) contains an elaborate system of retaining walls, which are shown partly in figure 69. At first a retaining wall was built immediately in front of the main kiva, which is now 5 feet high outside. Apparently this did not serve the purpose intended, for another and much heavier wall was built immediately next to it. This wall is 4 feet thick, flush on top and inside, but 10 feet high outside. At half its height it has a step back of 6 inches. It would seem that even this heavy construction did not suffice, and still another wall was built outside of and next to it. This wall is nearly or quite as heavy as the one described, and its top is on the level of the foot of that wall, but it is 12 feet high outside. Something of the character of the site may be inferred from the arrangement of these walls, which have a combined vertical fall of 27 feet in a horizontal distance of less than 15 feet. The outer or lower wall has a series of very heavy timbers projecting from its face; these are placed irregularly. It should be noted that access to this village was from the bench on either side, and that it could not be reached from the front, where these walls occur. There are other walls on the lower slope, similarly reinforced.

A little to the right of the point where these retaining walls occur there is a room in which horizontal beams have been incorporated in the masonry. A similar use of timber occurs in ruin No. 16 and is shown in plate LX. Why timber should be used in this way is not clear. It may be that when the supply was placed on the ground the builders found that they had more timber than was needed for a roof and used the excess in the wall rather than bring up more stone. The posts which were placed vertically and built into the wall were always short; perhaps they were fragments or ends cut from roofing timbers that were found to be too long. In many instances they failed to hold the walls, and possibly the pit holes in sloping rock, which are numerous on some sites, indicate places where this expedient was formerly employed.

It is singular that the necessity for such expedients did not develop the idea of a buttress. On this site such an expedient would have saved an immense amount of work. In only one place in the canyon was a buttress found. This was in the Casa Blanca ruin, shown in plate XLVII. There is no doubt that in this place the buttress was used with a full knowledge of its principles, and but little doubt that the idea was imported at a late, perhaps the latest, period in the occupancy of that site. Had it been known before, it would have been used in other places where there was great need for it, not so much to prevent the slipping of walls as to supersede the construction of walls 4 feet thick or more, and to strengthen outside walls which were likely to give way at any time from the outward thrust upon them.

Altogether the constructive expedients employed in De Chelly suggest the introduction of plans and methods adapted to other regions and other conditions into a new region with different requirements, and that occupancy of the latter region did not continue long enough to conform the methods to the new conditions.

KIVAS OR SACRED CHAMBERS

The kivas, or estufas as they formerly were called, are sacred chambers in which the civil and religious affairs of the tribe are transacted, and they also form a place of resort, or club, as it were, for the men. Their functions are many and varied, but as this subject has already been discussed at length[1] it need not be enlarged upon here. In Tusayan the kivas are rectangular and separated from the houses; in Zuñi and in some other pueblos they are also rectangular, but are incorporated in the house clusters—a feature doubtless brought about by the repressive policy of the Spanish monks. In some of the pueblos, as in Taos, they are circular, and in many of the older ruins the same form is found. In the large ruins of Chaco canyon the kivas occur in groups arranged along the inner side of the rooms; always, where the ground plan is such as to permit it, arranged on the border of an inner court. In Canyon de Chelly the kivas are always circular and are placed generally on the outer edge of the settlement, which is usually the front.

As the function of the kivas is principally a religious one, they are found only in permanent villages where religious ceremonies were performed. They are never found in subordinate settlements, or farming villages, or outlooks, unless such settlements came to be inhabited all the year—in other words, until they became permanent villages. The habits and requirements of the Pueblo people make it essential that a permanent village should have one or more kivas, and we have in the presence of these structures a criterion by which the character of a village or ruin may be determined. As the kivas in De Chelly are always circular, they can generally be easily distinguished.

The circular kiva is unquestionably a survival in architecture—a relic of the time when the Pueblo people dwelt in circular lodges or huts—and its use in conjunction with a rectangular system entailed many difficulties and some awkward expedients to overcome them. The main problem, how to use the two systems together, was solved by inclosing the circular chamber in a rectangular cell, and this expedient aided in the solution of the hardly less important problem of roofing. The roof of the kiva was the roof of the chamber that inclosed it.

It seems to have been a common requirement throughout the pueblo country that the kiva should be wholly or partly underground. So strong was this requirement in Tusayan that the occurrence of natural clefts and fissures in the rock of the mesa top has dictated the location of the kivas often at some distance from the houses. But in De Chelly there were some sites where the requirement could not be filled without extensive rock excavation wholly beyond the power of the builders.

---

[1] 8th Ann. Rept. Bur. Eth., "A study of Pueblo architecture in Tusayan and Cibola," by Victor Mindeleff; Washington, 1891.

Here then it seems that other requirements were strong enough to overcome the ceremonial necessity for partly subterranean structures, for examples of that kind are comparatively rare. In all of the ruins on the canyon bottom the requirement could be filled, and as many of the villages on defensive sites were constructed after the site itself had been partly filled up with loose débris, it could also be filled in those cases. There are also instances where the bottom of the kiva rests directly on the rock, while outside the walls the site was covered deep with artificial débris. But it would be difficult to determine what was the surface of the ground when the kiva was in use.

The size and character of the kivas in De Chelly, and their relations to the other rooms about them, are shown in the ground plans preceding. Some have walls still standing to a height of 6 feet above the ground, but this could not have been the total height. Dr H. C. Yarrow, U. S. A., in 1874 examined one of the five large circular kivas in Taos. He states[1] that it was 25 or 30 feet in diameter, arched above, and 20 feet high. Around the wall, 2 feet from the ground, there was a hard earthen bench, and in the center a fireplace about 2 by 3 feet.

Entrance to the kivas is invariably from the roof by a ladder. This appears to be a ceremonial requirement. Doorways at the ground level are not only unknown, but

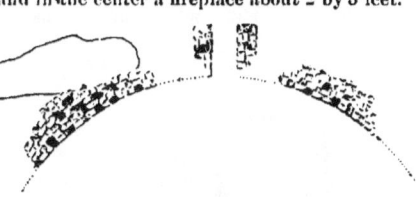

FIG. 70—Part of a kiva in ruin No. 31.

also impracticable; but in De Chelly there are some puzzling features which might easily be mistaken for such doorways. The principal kiva in the ruin, which occurs at the point marked 10 on the map, and described above (page 123, figure 24), is on the edge of the ledge, and its outer wall is so close as to make a passage difficult, although not impossible. At the point where the curved wall comes nearest the cliff there is a narrow gap or opening, not more than 15 inches wide. In front of this there appears to be a little platform on the sloping rock, 2 feet long, 10 inches wide, and now about a foot high. At first sight this would be taken for a doorway so arranged that access to the kiva could be obtained only from below; but a closer examination shows that this was probably only what remains of a chimney-like structure, such as those described later.

In ruin 31 there is another example. The kiva here was about 20 feet in diameter, with rather thin walls smoothly plastered inside. On the inner side the walls are from 3 to 5 feet high; outside they are generally flush with the ground. The kiva is not a true circle, but is slightly elongated north and south. On the south side, nearest the edge of the ledge, there is an opening, shown in figure 70. The opening is 6 feet 3 inches

[1] Wheeler Survey Reports, vol. vii. Archæology, p. 327.

wide, and the ends of the curved walls terminate in smoothly finished surfaces. In front of it there are remains of two walls, about a foot apart, and so arranged as to form an apparent passageway into the interior of the kiva. These seem to be a kind of platform, like that just described, but close inspection shows the walls, which can be traced to within 6 inches of the inner wall of the kiva. This also may be the remains of a chimney-like structure. There are other points in the canyon where the same feature occurs, but in none of them is the evidence of an opening or doorway more definite than in the examples described.

The masonry of the kivas is always as good as that of any other structure on the site, and generally much better. The walls are usually massive; sometimes they are 3 feet thick in the upper part and 4 feet in the lower portion, where the bench occurs. In a few cases the kiva has an upper or second story, but when this occurs no attempt is made to preserve the circular form, and the upper rooms are really rectangular with much rounded corners. Plate XLIX shows a second-story kiva wall in Mummy Cave ruin, and plate LXIII one in ruin No. 10 in De Chelly.

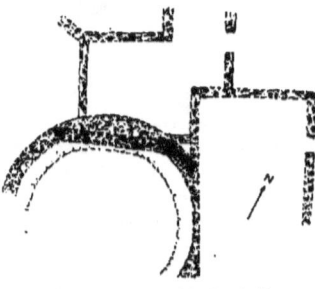

The latter occurs over the principal kiva', and the walls which are still standing on the north and west sides are approximately straight, but the corners are much rounded. Figure 71 is a detailed plan of part of the kiva, showing the arrangement of the upper walls. The kiva walls are about 18 inches thick. On the north side the upper wall is supported by a heavy beam, part of which is still in place. Under the north-east corner of the upper room

FIG. 71—Plan of part of a kiva in ruin No. 10.

there is a little triangular space formed by a short connecting wall, shown on the plan. This is really a flying wall, covering only the upper portion of the space, and its purpose is not clear, as the opening left is not large enough to permit the passage of a person, and was available only from the second story.

Apparently the greatest care was bestowed on the construction and finish of the kivas. The exterior of the circular wall is often rough and unfinished, but this is probably because the whole structure was generally inclosed within rectangular walls. The interior was plastered, often with a number of coats. The southern kiva in ruin No. 10 shows a number of these on its interior surface, applied one after another, and now forming a plastering nearly three-quarters of an inch thick. In its section 18 distinct coats can be counted, separated one from the other by a thin film of smoke-blackened surface. The kiva in ruin No. 16 has 4 or 5 coats, that in ruin No. 31 shows at least 8. In the last example the last coat was not decorated, but some of the underlying ones were.

Kivas are used principally in the autumn and winter, when the farming season is over and the ceremonies and dances take place. It is probable, therefore, that each coat of plaster means at least a year in the history of the kiva, which would indicate that some of the sites were occupied about twenty years. But Mr Frank H. Cushing has observed in Zuñi a ceremony, part of which is the refinishing of the kiva interior, and this occurs only once in four years. This would give a maximum occupancy of about eighty years to some of the kivas; the ruins as a whole would hardly justify an hypothesis of a longer occupancy than this. In Tusayan the interior of the kiva is plastered by the women once every year at the feast of Powamu (the fructifying moon).

The kivas are seldom true circles, being usually elongated one way or another. Some instances occur which are rectangular, such as the room shown in figure 19, which was apparently a kiva. Nordenskiöld[1] illustrates an example which appears to have been oval by design,

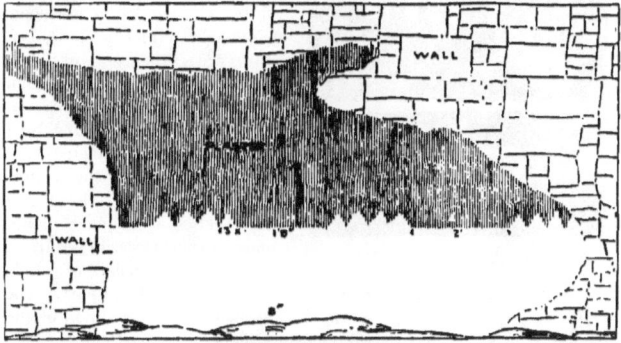

FIG. 73—Kiva decoration in white.

differing in this respect from anything found in De Chelly. Most of the kivas have an interior bench, about a foot wide and 2 feet above the floor. This bench is sometimes continuous around the whole interior, sometimes extends only partly around. Wherever the chimney-like structure is attached to a kiva the bench is omitted or broken at that point. The kiva wall on the floor level is always continuous except before the chimney-like feature. The most elaborate system of benches and buttresses seen in the canyon occurs in the principal kiva of the Mummy Cave ruin. This is shown in the ground plan, figure 16, and also in figures 82 and 83. In the ruins of the Mancos, Nordenskiöld found kivas in which this feature is carried much further. He illustrates[2] an example with a complete bench regularly divided into six equal parts by an equal number of buttresses or pillars (properly pilasters) extending out flush with the front of the bench. This is said

[1] Cliff Dwellers of the Mesa Verde, p. 63, fig. 36.
[2] Loc. cit., figs. 6 and 7, pp. 15-16.

to be a typical example, to which practically all the kivas conform. It has also the chimney-like structure, to be described later. Like the

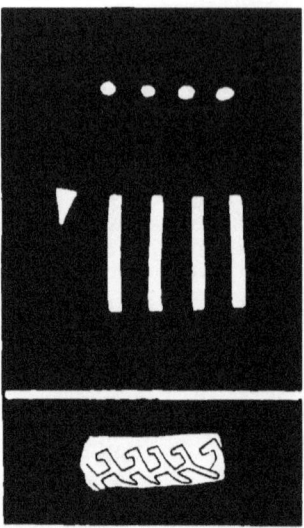

rectangular kivas of Tusayan the circular structures of De Chelly have little niches in the walls. Probably these were places of deposit for certain paraphernalia used in the ceremonies.

Some of the kivas have an interior decoration consisting of a band with points. Figure 72 shows an example that occurs in ruin No. 10 in De Chelly, in the north kiva. The band, done in white, is about 18 inches below the bench, and its top is broken at intervals into groups of points rising from it, four points in each group. In the north kiva the interior wall is decorated by a series of vertical bands in white. One series occurs on the vertical face of the bench; the bands are 2 inches wide and 8 inches apart. Another series occurs on the wall, and consists of bands

FIG. 73.—Pictograph in white.

2½ to 3 inches wide, about 2 feet high and 12 to 14 inches apart. The bands were observed only on the southern and western sides of the kiva, but originally there may have been others on the north and east.

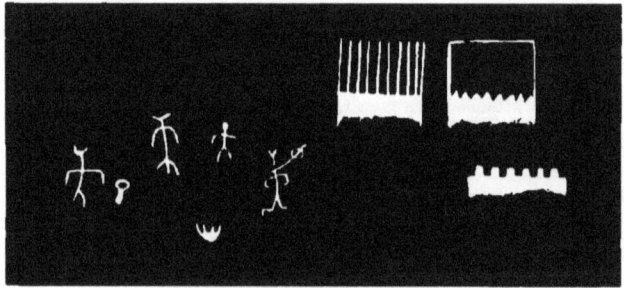

FIG. 74.—Markings on cliff wall, ruin No. 57.

In ruin No. 4 there is a similar series of bars, but in this instance they occur on the cliff wall back of the rooms. They are shown in figure 73.

FIG. 75.—Decorative band in kiva in Mummy Cave ruin.

FIG. 76—Designs employed in decorative band.

There are four bars or upright bands, done in white paint, and surmounted by four round dots or spots. To the left of the four bars, level with their tops, there is a small triangle, also in white. The bars are 30 inches long and 4 inches wide. The upper dots are nearly 2 feet above the tops of the bars. It is evident that this figure was designed to be seen from a distance. Figure 74 shows some markings on the cliff wall back of ruin No. 57.

Examples almost identical with those shown here are abundant in the Mancos ruins. It is probable that they are of ceremonial rather than of decorative origin, and in this connection it may be stated that Mr Frank H. Cushing has observed in Zuñi the ceremony of marking the sides of a kiva hatchway with white bars closely resembling those shown in figure 73. This ceremony occurs once in four years, and the purpose of the marks is said to be to indicate the cardinal directions. In the ceremonials of the Pueblo Indians it is necessary to know where the cardinal points are; a prayer, for instance, is often addressed to the north, west, south, and east, and when such ceremonials were performed in a circular chamber some means by which the direction could be determined was essential.

In the principal kiva in Mummy Cave ruin, however, there is a painted band on the front of the bench which appears to be really an attempt at decoration. Over the white there is a band 4 or 5 inches wide, consisting of a meander done in red. This is shown in figure 75, and in detail in figure 76. The design is similar to that used today. Its importance arises not so much from this as from the fact that it is difficult to regard this as other than ornamentation, and the Pueblo architect had not yet reached the stage of ornamented construction. The ruins in the Mancos canyon and the Mesa Verde country obviously represent a later stage in development than those in De Chelly, yet nowhere in that region do we find the counterpart of the decoration in Mummy Cave kiva. Bands with points occur, sometimes on walls of rectangular rooms. One such is illustrated by Chapin,[1] who also shows a variety of the meander, treated, however, as a pictograph and

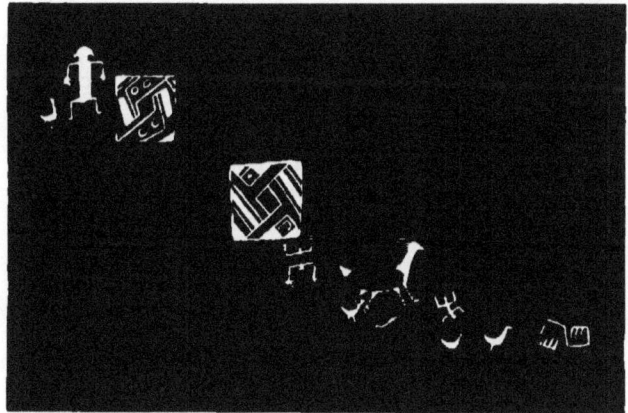

FIG. 77—Pictographs in Canyon de Chelly.

without reference to its decorative value. Similar bands are shown also by Nordenskiöld,[2] but always with three points, instead of four, which were done in red. Figure 77 shows some pictographs somewhat resembling the Mancos examples. These occur at the point marked 1 on the map, in connection with a small storage cist already described.

No kiva has been found in De Chelly with a roof in place. Nearly all of them are inclosed in rectangular chambers, and it seems more than probable that the roofing of the kiva was simply the roofing of the inclosing chamber. As a rule the inclosing rectangular walls were erected at the same time as the kiva proper, and the outside of the inner circular wall was not finished at all. In a few instances the space

[1] Land of the Cliff Dwellers. Illustration, pp. 147, 152.
[2] Cliff Dwellers of the Mesa Verde. figs. 6, 7, 76, 77, and 78.

between the outer rectangular and inner circular wall was filled in solid, or perhaps was so constructed, but usually the walls are separate and distinct.

CHIMNEY-LIKE STRUCTURES

There are peculiar structures found in some of the ruins, whose use and object are not clear. Reference has already been made to them in the descriptions of several ruins, and for want of a better name they have been designated chimney-like structures. At the time that they were examined they were supposed to be new, and the first hypothesis formed was that they were abortive chimneys, but further examination showed that this idea was not tenable. Subsequently Nordenskiöld's book on the Cliff Dwellers of the Mesa Verde was published, and it appears therefrom that this

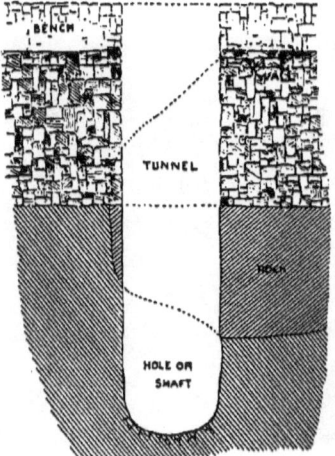

feature is very common in the region treated; so common as to constitute the type.

Figure 78 is a plan of one of these structures which occurs in ruin No. 15 in Canyon de Chelly. This ruin has already been described in detail (page 118). The chimney-like structure is attached to a rectangular room with rounded corners, which is supposed to have been a kiva, and which was two stories high. Excavation revealed the floor level about $7\frac{1}{2}$ feet below where the roof was placed. In the center of the south wall there is an opening 1.5 feet high and eighty-five one-hundredths of a foot (10.2

FIG. 78—Plan of chimney-like structure in ruin No. 15.

inches) wide. The south wall is built over a large bowlder, and a tunnel or opening passes under this to a rounded vertical shaft, about a foot in diameter, which opens to the air. This perhaps is better shown in the section (figure 79). At first sight this would appear to be a chimney, but there are several objections to the idea. The interior of the shaft is not blackened by smoke, and while the tunnel is somewhat smoke-stained, the deposit is not so pronounced as on the walls of the room. The front of the tunnel in the room has a lintel composed of a single stick about an inch in diameter, as shown in the section. The roof of the tunnel was the underside of the large bowlder mentioned, and the stick lintel was of no use except to show that no fire could have been built under it. The roof of the southern end of the tunnel, where it opens into the shaft, is considerably lower than at the other end. The floor of the tunnel and the sides were smoothly plastered, but the plastering does not appear to have been subjected to the action of fire.

The interior of the room, like the circular kivas already described, appears to have been plastered with a number of successive coats, all except the last being heavily stained by smoke. If the structure were a chimney, it was a dismal failure. The tunnel was made at the time the wall was erected, and passes under the bowlder over which the wall was built. A little east of the opening, inside the room, the bowlder shows through the wall, projecting slightly beyond its face.

Outside of the room the corner of the bowlder was chipped off, as shown on the plan, to permit the rounding of the shaft, the east, west, and south sides of which were built up with small pieces of stone, a

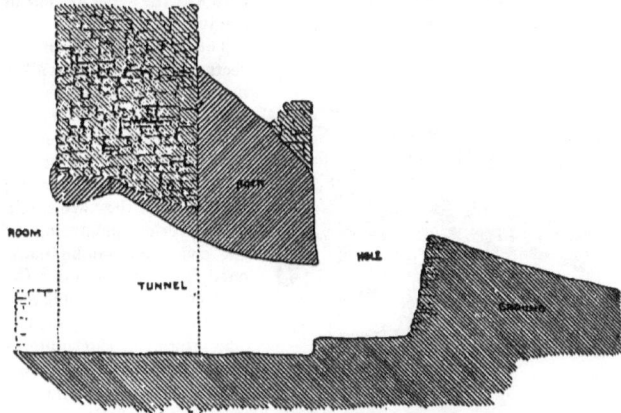

FIG. 79—Section of chimney-like structure in ruin No. 15.

kind of lining of masonry. There was also an outside structure of masonry, but how high above the ground it extended can not now be determined. A small fragment of this masonry is still left on the upper surface of the bowlder and is shown in the section.

Figure 80 is a plan of another example, which is attached to the circular kiva in ruin No. 16. This ruin is described on page 129. The kiva had an interior bench and the floor is 2 feet above its top. On the south side nearest the cliff edge the bench is interrupted to give place to a structure much like that described above. In this case, however, there was no convenient bowlder, and the roof of the tunnel has broken down so that the method of support can not be accurately determined. Probably it consisted of slabs of rock, as the span is small, and a number of large flat stones were removed from the tunnel in excavating.

The top of the tunnel is on the level of the top of the bench, as shown in figure 81, which is a vertical section. An inspection of the plan will show that the circular wall of the kiva is complete and that the inclosing rectangular wall was added later. The shaft was built at a still later period, and the line or junction marking its inner surface shows plainly in the interior of the tunnel. The general view of the ruin (plate LI) shows the exterior of the shaft, and the horizontal timbers on which the masonry is supported are shown in plate LII.

In front of the tunnel a flat piece of stone was placed on the floor, and in front of this again, about 2 feet from the mouth of the tunnel, there was an upright mass of masonry composed of stone and mud, and forming a curtain or screen before the opening. The original height of this structure was the same as that of the interior bench.

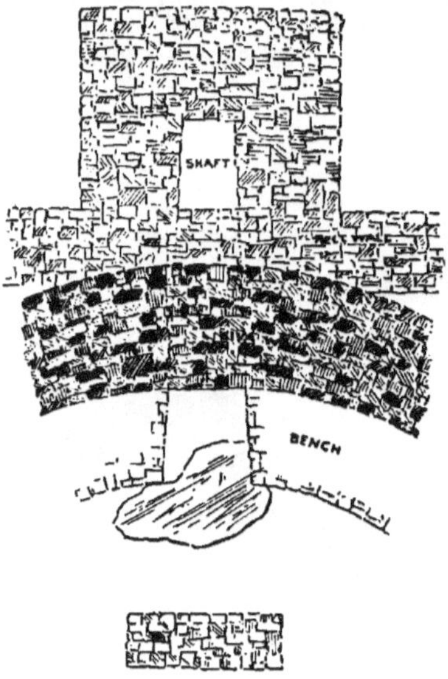

The inner surface of the rectangular inclosing wall is marked by a line in the interior of the tunnel. Inside of this line, toward the center of the kiva, the stones composing the wall are large; outside of it they are small. The interior plastering of the kiva is not smoke-blackened, but the coat next the surface is stained, as is also the third coat underneath. The interior of the tunnel is not much smoke-blackened, but it appears probable that part of its roof fell while the structure was still in use, as there are a number of little cavities in the masonry above its roof level filled with soot. A similar effect might result from leaks or cavities between the flat roofing stones. In excavating the tunnel a number of large lumps of clay were found in it, and there is no doubt that they formed part of the roof. Some of these had considerable quantities of grass mixed into them or stuck to the clay on one side. Apparently dry grass was used in the construction. A large fire could not have been built within the tunnel.

FIG. 80—Plan of chimney-like structure in ruin No. 10.

The principal kiva in Mummy Cave ruin has an elaborate structure of the kind under discussion. Figure 82 shows a plan of this kiva, of which a general view has already been given (figure 75). The bench

extended only partly around the interior, which had a continuous surface at the floor level, except on the southwest. At this point it is
interrupted to give place to an elaborate chimney-like structure. Figure
83 is a general view.

The wall surface on the southern side of the kiva has been extended
inward, as shown on the plan by a lighter shaded area. This was done
at some period subsequent to the completion of the kiva, but whether
it had any connection with the chimney-like structure could not be
determined. The curtain or screen before the opening, which seems to
be an invariable feature, is shown in both figures.

In this example the tunnel does not pass through the masonry as in
those previously described, but occurs in the form of a covered trough,
shown in the illustration with the covering removed. It occupies the
middle third of a large recess in the main wall of the kiva, and is con-

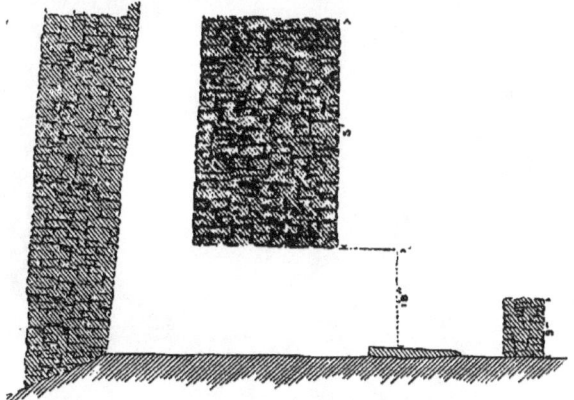

FIG. 81—Section of chimney-like structure in ruin No. 16.

nected at its outer end with a vertical square shaft about a foot wide.
This shaft is separated from the recess above the bench level by a wall
only a few inches thick, composed of a single layer of stones. That
portion of it which is above the tunnel is supported by a single round
stick of wood, as shown in figure 83. The south or inner opening
of the tunnel is reduced to two-thirds of the width elsewhere by a
framing composed of bundles of sticks bound together with withes and
heavily coated with mud mortar. This was not placed flush with the
inner face, but a few inches back, and the whole structure gives an
effect of unusual neatness and good workmanship.

At various other points in the canyons examples of chimney-like
structures occur, none, however, constructed on the elaborate plan of
that last described. Two examples were found in the large rooms west
of the tower in the central portion of Mummy Cave ruin, and these are

especially worthy of attention because they are attached to rectangular rooms, which there is no reason to suppose were kivas. The first room appears to have had a shaft only, without a niche or recess; the second room west of the tower had a recess and a rounded shaft, while the third room had neither recess nor shaft.

The usual form of this feature is that shown in figures 80 and 81, and consists only of a tunnel and shaft. There are not many examples in the canyons: altogether there may be a dozen now visible, but excavations in the village ruins would doubtless reveal others. Except the two in Mummy Cave ruin last mentioned, and some doubt-

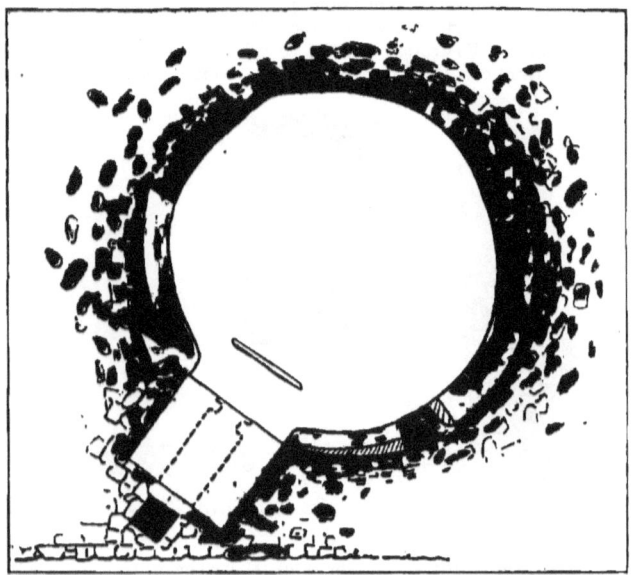

Fig. 82—Plan of the principal kiva in Mummy Cave ruin.

ful examples to be described later, they occur always as attachments to kivas, never to houses. Some of them, like the Mummy Cave example, were certainly built at the same time as the kivas, of which they formed a part; others were added to kivas after those structures had been completed and used.

The kiva in Casa Blanca ruin (shown in figure 14) appears to have had an appendage of this sort, not constructed after the usual manner, but added outside the rectangular wall and composed of mud or adobe. At three other places in the lower ruin these structures are found, all constructed of mud or adobe and all attached to adobe walls. It is

FIG. 82.—Chimney-like structure in Mummy Cave ruin.

doubtful whether these three examples should be classed with the preceding, but as they may have been used in the same manner they should be mentioned here. Another doubtful example occurs in the upper part of the same ruin and has already been described (page 110). It was constructed of stone at some time subsequent to the completion of the wall against which it rests.

Over twenty ago Mr W. H. Holmes found a structure in Mancos canyon which it now appears may be of this type. He illustrates it by a ground plan and thus describes it:

> The most striking feature of this structure [ruin] is the round room, which occurs about the middle of the ruin and inside of a large rectangular apartment. . . . Its walls are not high and not entirely regular, and the inside is curiously fashioned with offsets and box-like projections. It is plastered smoothly and bears considerable evidence of having been used, although I observed no traces of fire. The entrance to this chamber is rather extraordinary, and further attests the peculiar importance attached to it by the builders and their evident desire to secure it from all possibility of intrusion. A walled and covered passageway of solid masonry, 10 feet of which is still intact, leads from an outer chamber through the small intervening apartments into the circular one. It is possible that this originally extended to the outer wall and was entered from the outside. If so, the person desiring to visit the estufa [kiva] would have to enter an aperture about 22 inches high by 30 wide and crawl in the most abject manner possible through a tube-like passageway nearly 20 feet in length. My first impression was that this peculiarly constructed doorway was a precaution against enemies and that it was probably the only means of entrance to the interior of the house, but I am now inclined to think this hardly probable, and conclude that it was rather designed to render a sacred chamber as free as possible from profane intrusion.[1]

In this example the tunnel was much larger than usual and the vertical shaft, if there were one, has been so much broken down that it is no longer distinguishable. Nordenskiöld mentions a considerable number of kivas with this attachment, and one which is described and figured is said to be a type of all the kivas in that region, but an inspection of his ground plans shows more kivas without this feature than with it. In his description of a small ruin in Cliff canyon he speaks of—

> . . . a circular room still in a fair state of preservation. The wall that lies nearest the precipice is for the most part in ruins; the rest of the room is well preserved. After about half a meter of dust and rubbish had been removed, we were able to ascertain that the wall formed a cylinder 4.3 meters in diameter. The thickness of the wall is throughout considerable, and varies, the spaces between the points where the cylinder touches the walls of adjoining rooms[2] having been filled up with masonry. The height of the room is 2 meters. The roof has long since fallen in, and only one or two beams are left among the rubbish. To a height of 1.2 meters from the floor the wall is perfectly even and has the form of a cylinder, or rather of a truncate cone, as it leans slightly inward. The upper portion, on the other hand, is divided by six deep niches into the same number of pillars. The floor is of clay

---

[1] 10th Ann. Rept. U. S. Geol. and Geog. Survey of the Territories, F. V. Hayden in charge (Washington, 1878); report on the "Ancient ruins of Southwestern Colorado," by W. H. Holmes; p. 395, pl. xxxvii.

[2] In the ground plan given there is no point shown where the walls of the kiva touch adjoining rooms.

hard, and perfectly even. Near the center is a round depression or hole, five-tenths of a meter deep and eight-tenths of a meter in diameter. This hole was entirely full of white ashes. It was undoubtedly the hearth. Between the hearth and the outer wall stands a narrow, curved wall, eight-tenths of a meter high. Behind this wall, in the same plane as the door, a rectangular opening, 1 meter high and six-tenths of a meter broad, has been constructed in the outer wall. This opening forms the mouth of a narrow passage or tunnel of rectangular shape, which runs 1.8 meters in a horizontal direction and then goes straight upward, out into the open air. The tunnel lies under one of the six niches, which is somewhat deeper than the others. The walls are built of carefully hewn blocks of sandstone, the inner surface being perfectly smooth and lined with a thin, yellowish plaster. On closer examination of this plaster it is found to consist of several thin layers, each of them black with soot. The plaster has evidently been repeatedly restored as the walls became blackened with smoke. A few smaller niches and holes in the walls, irregularly scattered here and there, have presumably served as places of deposit for different articles; a bundle of pieces of hide, tied with a string, was found in one of them. The lower part of the wall, to a height of four-tenths of a meter, is painted dark red around the whole room. This red paint projects upward in triangular points, arranged in threes, and above them is a row of small round dots of red. . . . Circular rooms, built and arranged on exactly the same plan as that described above, reappear with exceedingly slight variations in size and structure in every cliff dwelling except the very smallest ones. . . . The number of estufas [kivas] varies in proportion to the size of the buildings and the number of rooms. . . . [The ruin described contained two kivas.] . . . The description of the first estufa applies in every respect to the second, with the single exception that the whole wall is coated with yellow plaster without any red painting. The wall between the hearth and the singular passage or tunnel described above is replaced by a large slab of stone set on end. It is difficult to say for what purpose this tunnel has been constructed and the slab of stone or the wall erected in front of it. As I have mentioned above, this arrangement is found in all the estufas.[1]

The general similarity between the kivas of De Chelly and those of the Mesa Verde region will be apparent from the above description. It should be added that in the section which accompanies it the roof of the tunnel appears to be supported by a series of small cross sticks, although no information on this point is afforded by the text. The examples which occur in De Chelly are apparently much ruder and more primitive than those of the Mancos, and only one of them approaches the latter in finish and elaboration.

In another place [2] Nordenskiöld mentions an example in which two small sticks were incorporated in the masonry of the upper part of the tunnel in a diagonal position. From this he rejects Holmes' explanation that the passageway was used as an entrance to the kiva, nor does he find the chimney hypothesis satisfactory. He states, further, that the use of this feature as a ventilator seems highly improbable. In one place he found the curtain or screen constructed not of masonry, but—

. . . of thick stakes, driven into the ground close to each other, and fastened together at the top with osiers. On the side nearest to the hearth this wooden screen was covered with a thick layer of mortar, probably to protect the timber from the heat.[3]

[1] Cliff Dwellers of the Mesa Verde, pp. 15-17, figs. 6 and 7.
[2] Loc. cit., p. 32.
[3] Loc. cit., p. 79.

As stated elsewhere, the first hypothesis formed in the field as to the purpose of these chimney-like structures was that they were abortive chimneys, but this was found untenable. The next hypothesis, formed also in the field, was that they were ceremonial in origin and use, but why they should connect with the open air is not clear. If we could assume that they were ventilators, the problem would be solved, but it is a far cry from pueblo architecture to ventilation; a stride, as it were, over many centuries. Ventilation according to this method—the introduction of fresh air on a low level, striking on a screen a little distance from the inlet and being thereby evenly distributed over the whole chamber—is a development in house architecture reached only by our own civilization within the last few decades.

If the shaft and tunnel were in place, however, the screen might follow as a matter of necessity. Entrance to the kivas is always through the roof, a ceremonial requirement quite as rigidly adhered to today among the Pueblos as it was formerly among their ancestors. The same opening which gives access also provides an exit to the smoke from the fire, which is invariably placed in the center of the kiva below it. This fire is a ceremonial rather than a necessary feature, for in the coldest weather the presence of a dozen men in a small chamber, air-tight except for a small opening in the roof, very soon raises the temperature to an uncomfortable degree, and the air becomes so fetid that a white man, not accustomed to it, is nauseated in half an hour or less. Such are the conditions in the modern kivas of Tusayan. In the smaller structures of De Chelly they must have been worse. The fire is, therefore, made very small and always of very dry wood, so as to diminish as far as possible the output of smoke. Frank H. Cushing states that in certain ceremonials which occur in the kivas it is considered very necessary that the fire should burn brightly and that the flame should rise straight from it. If this requirement prevailed in De Chelly, a screen of some sort would surely follow the construction of a shaft and tunnel.

More or less smoke is generally present in the kivas when a fire is burning, notwithstanding the care taken to prevent it. That a similar condition prevailed in the kivas of De Chelly is shown by the smoke-blackened plaster of the interiors. In some cases there was a room over the kivas which must have increased the difficulty very much. There can be little doubt that the chimney-like structures were not chimneys, and no doubt at all that they did provide an efficient means of ventilation, no matter what the intention of the builders may have been. When we know more of the ceremonials of the Pueblo Indians, and when extensive excavations have developed the various types and varieties of these structures in the ruins, we may be able to determine their object and use.

TRADITIONS

It has often been stated concerning some given ruin or region that the traditions of the present inhabitants of the country do not reach them. In the case of Canyon de Chelly the same statement might be made, for more than 99 Navaho in 100, when asked what became of the people who built the old houses in De Chelly, will state that a great wind arose and swept them all away, which is equivalent to saying that they do not know. There is a tradition in the Navaho tribe, however, now very difficult to get, as it is confined to a few of the old priests. It recites the occupancy of the canyon before the Navaho obtained possession of it, but, curiously enough, this period is placed after the Spanish invasion. It is even asserted that there were monks in De Chelly, and Mummy Cave, Casa Blanca, and one other ruin have been pointed out as the places where they were stationed. No version of this tradition definite and complete enough ·for publication could be obtained by the writer, but Dr Washington Matthews, U. S. A., whose knowledge of Navaho myths and traditions is so great that it can almost be termed exhaustive, has obtained one and doubtless will publish it.

The Hopi or Moki Indians, whose villages are some three days' journey to the west, have also very definite traditions bearing on the occupancy of De Chelly.[1] This tribe, like others, is composed of a number of related clans who reached their present location from various directions and at various times; but, with a few exceptions, each of these clans claims to have lived at one time or another in Canyon de Chelly. How much truth there is in these claims can be determined only when the entire region has been examined and thoroughly studied. In the meantime it will probably be safe to assume that some, at least, of the ruins in De Chelly are of Hopi origin.

CONCLUSIONS

To understand the ruins so profusely scattered over the ancient pueblo country we must have some knowledge of the conditions under which their inhabitants lived. Were nothing at all known, however, we would be justified in inferring, from the results that have been produced, a similarity of conditions with those prevailing among the pueblo tribes, both formerly and now; and all the evidence so far obtained would support that inference. There is no warrant whatever for the old assumption that the "cliff dwellers" were a separate race, and the cliff dwellings must be regarded as only a phase of pueblo architecture.

More or less speculation regarding the origin of pueblo culture is the usual and perhaps proper accompaniment of nearly all treatises bearing on that subject. Early writers on the Aztec culture, aided by a vague tradition of that tribe that they came from the north, pushed the point of emigration farther and farther and still farther north, until finally the pueblo country was reached. Pueblo ruins are even now known locally as "Aztec ruins." Logically the inhabited villages should be classed as "Aztec colonies," and such classification was not unusual when the country came into the possession of the United States some fifty years ago.

[1] A résumé of the Hopi traditions was prepared by the writer from material collected by the late A. M. Stephen, and published as chapter iii of "A study of Pueblo architecture," op. cit.

As our knowledge of the pueblo culture increased, a gradual separation between the old and the new took place, and we have as an intermediate hypothesis many "Aztec ruins," but no "Aztec colonies." Finally, as a result of still further knowledge, the ruins and the inhabited pueblos are again brought together; several lines of investigation have combined to show the continuity of the old and the present culture, and the connection may be considered well established. But there is still a disposition to regard the cliff ruins as a thing apart. The old idea of a separate race of cliff dwellers now finds little credence, but the cliff ruins are almost universally explained as the results of extraordinary, primitive, or unusual causes.

The intimate relation between the savage and his physical environment has already been alluded to. Nature, or that part of nature which we term physical environment, enters into and becomes part of the life of the savage in a way and to an extent that we can hardly conceive. A change of physical environment does not produce an immediate change in the man or in his arts, but in time such must inevitably result. Twenty-five years ago the savage of the plains and the savage of the pueblo country were regarded as distinct races, "as different from each other as light is from darkness;" yet the differences which appeared so striking at first have become fewer and fewer as our knowledge of the Indian tribes increased, and those which remain today can almost all be attributed to a difference in physical environment.

Linguistic researches have shown the close connection which exists between the Hopi (Moki) and some of the plains (or so called "wild") Indians. There is no doubt that at the time of the Spanish discovery, some three hundred and fifty years ago, the Hopi were quite as far advanced as the other pueblo tribes, and the conclusion is irresistible that since it may reasonably be inferred that one tribe has made the change from a nomadic to a sedentary life, other tribes also may have done so. We may go even farther than this, and assume that a nomadic tribe driven into the pueblo country, or drifting into it, would remain as before under the direct influence of its physical environment, although the environment would be a new one. Granting this, and the element of time, and we will have no difficulty with the origin of pueblo architecture.

The complete adaptation of pueblo architecture to the country in which it is found has been commented on. Ordinarily such adaptation would imply two things—origin within the country, and a long period of time for development—but there are several factors that must be taken into consideration. If the architecture did not originate in the country where it is found it would almost certainly bear traces of former conditions. Such survivals are common in all arts, and instances of it are so common in architecture that no examples need be cited. Only one of these survivals has been found in pueblo architecture, but that one is very instructive; it is the presence of circular chambers in groups of rectangular rooms, which occur in certain regions. These chambers are called estufas or kivas and are the council houses and temples of the people, in which the governmental and religious affairs of the tribe are transacted. It is owing to their religious connection that the form has been preserved to the present day, carrying with it the record of the time when the people lived in round chambers or huts.

In opposition to the hypothesis of local origin it might be stated that there is no evidence of forms intermediate in development. The oldest remains of pueblo architecture known are but little different from recent examples. But it must be borne in mind that pueblo architecture is of a very low order, so low that it hardly comes within a definition of architecture as an art, as opposed to a craft. Except for a few examples, some of which have already been mentioned, it was strictly utilitarian in character; the savage had certain needs to supply, and he supplied them in the easiest and most direct manner and with material immediately at hand. The whole pueblo country is covered with the remains of single rooms and groups of rooms, put up to meet some immediate necessity. Some of these may have been built centuries ago, some are only a few years or a few months old, yet the structures do not differ from one another; nor, on the other hand, does the similarity imply that the builder of the oldest example knew less or more than his descendant today—both utilized the material at hand and each accomplished his purpose in the easiest way. In both cases the result is so rude that no sound inference of sequence can be drawn from the study of individual examples, but in the study of large aggregations of rooms we find some clues.

The aggregation of many single rooms into one great structure was produced by causes which have been discussed. It must not be forgotten that the unit of pueblo construction is the single room, even in the large, many-storied villages. This unit is often quite as rude in modern work as in ancient, and both modern and ancient examples are very close to the result which would be produced by any Indian tribe who came into the country and were left free to work out their own ideas. Starting with this unit the whole system of pueblo architecture is a natural product of the country in which it is found and the conditions of life known to have affected the people by whom it was practiced.

Granting the local origin of pueblo architecture it would appear at first sight that a very long period of time must have elapsed between the erection of the first rude rooms and the building of the many-storied pueblos, yet the evidence now available—that derived from the ruins themselves, documentary evidence, and traditions—all suggest that such was not necessarily the case. As a record of events, or rather of a sequence of events, tradition, when unsupported, has practically no value; but as a picture of life and of the conditions under which a people lived it is very instructive and full of suggestions, which, when followed out, often lead to the uncovering of valuable evidence. The traditions of the pueblo tribes record a great number of movements or

migrations from place to place, the statements being more or less
obscured by mythologic details and accounts of magic or miraculous
occurrences. When numbers of such movements are recorded, it is safe
to infer that the conditions dictating the occupancy of sites were unsta-
ble or even that the tribes were in a state of slow migration. When
this inference is supported by other evidence, it becomes much stronger,
and when the supporting evidence becomes more abundant, with no
discordant elements, the statement may be accepted as proved until
disproved.

The evident inferiority of the modern pueblos to some of the old ruins
has been urged as an argument against their connection. While degeneration in culture is yet to be proved, degeneration of some particular
art under adverse conditions, such as war, continued famine, or pesti-
lence, is not an uncommon incident in history, and it can be shown that
under the peculiar conditions which prevailed in the pueblo country
such degeneration would naturally take place. One of the peculiarities of pueblo architecture is that its results were obtained always by
the employment of the material immediately at hand. In the whole
pueblo region no instance is known where the material (other than timber) was transported to any distance; on the contrary, it was usually
obtained within a few feet of the site where it was used. Hence, it
comes about that difference in character of masonry is often only a
difference in material. Starting with a tribe or several tribes of plains
Indians, who came into the pueblo country, we should probably see
them at first building houses such as they were accustomed to build—
round huts of skin or brush, perhaps partly covered with earth, such
as were found all over middle and eastern United States. Supposing
the tribe to have been not very warlike in character and subsisting
principally by horticulture, these settlements would necessarily be confined to the vicinity of springs and to little valleys where the crops
could be grown. The general character of the country is arid in the
extreme, and only in favored spots is horticulture possible. In a very
short time these people would be forced to the use of stone for buildings, for the whole country is covered with tabular sandstone, often
broken up into blocks and flakes ready for immediate use without any
preparation whatever. Timber and brush could be procured only with
difficulty, and often had to be carried great distances.

It has been suggested that the rectangular form of rooms might have
been developed from the circular form by the crowding together upon
restricted sites of many circular chambers; but such a supposition
seems unnecessary. A structure of masonry designed to be roofed
would naturally be rectangular; in fact, the placing of a flat roof upon
a circular chamber was a problem whose solution was beyond the
ability of these people, as has already been shown. Along with this
advance, or perhaps preceding it, the social organization of the tribe,
or its division into clans and phratries, would manifest itself, and those
who "belong together" would build together. This requirement was a
very common one and was closely adhered to even a few years ago.

Although degeneration in arts is common enough, a peculiar condition prevailed in the pueblo region. So far as the architecture was concerned war and a hostile human environment produced not degeneration but development. This came about partly by reason of the peculiarities of the country, and partly through the methods of war. The term war is rather a misnomer in this connection, as it does not express the idea. The result was not brought about by armed bodies of men animated by hostile intentions or bent on extermination, although forays of this kind are too common in later pueblo history, but rather by predatory bands, bent on robbery and not indisposed to incidental killing. The pueblos, with their fixed habitations and their stores of food, were the natural prey of such bands, and they suffered, just as did, at a later period, the Mexican settlements on the Rio Grande, with their immense flocks of sheep. It was constant annoyance and danger, rather than war and pitched battles.

The pueblo country is exceptionally rich in building material suited to the knowledge and capacity of the pueblo builders. Had suitable material been less abundant, military knowledge would have developed and defensive structures would have been erected; but as such material could be obtained everywhere, and there was no lack of sites, almost if not quite equal to those occupied at any given time, the easiest and most natural thing to do was to move. Owing to the nature of the hostile pressure, such movements were generally gradual, not en masse; although there is no doubt that movements of the latter kind have sometimes taken place.

These conclusions are not based on a study of the ruins in Canyon de Chelly alone, which illustrate only one phase of the subject, but of all the pueblo remains, or rather of the remains so far as they are now known. They imply a rather sparsely settled country, occupied by a comparatively small number of tribes and subtribes, moving from place to place under the influence of various motives, some of which we know, others we can only surmise. It was a slow but practically constant migratory movement with no definite end or direction in view. The course of this movement in a geographical way does not as yet reveal a preponderance in any one direction; tribes and subtribes moved from east to west and from west to east, from north to south and from south to north, and many were irregular in their course, but the movements, so far as they can now be discerned, were all within a circumscribed area.

There is no evidence of any movement from without into the pueblo group, unless the close relation of the Hopi (Moki) language to the other Shoshonean dialects be such evidence, and none of a movement from within this area out of it, although such movements must have taken place, at least in the early history of the region. It must be borne in mind in this discussion that while we can assign approximate boundaries to the ancient pueblo region on the north, east, and west, no limit can as yet be fixed on the south. The arid country southward of Gila river and northward of the Mexican boundary would be a great

obstacle to a movement either north or south, but little as we know
about that region we do know that it was not an insurmountable obstacle. The Casas Grandes of Janos, in Chihuahua, closely resemble the
type of ruins on the Gila river, in Arizona, of which the best example
we now have is the well-known Casa Grande ruin. We know that
there are cliff ruins in the Sierra Madre, but beyond this we know
little. Concerning the immense region which stretches from Gila river
to the valley of Mexico, over 1300 miles in length, we know practically
nothing.

In that portion of the pueblo region lying within the United States
migratory movements have, as a rule, been confined to very small areas,
each linguistic family moving within its own circumscribed region.
Some instances of movement away from the home region have taken
place even in historic times, as, for example, the migration of a considerable band of Tewas from the Rio Grande to Tusayan, where they
now are, and moreover, this movement probably occurred en masse
and over a considerable distance; but there is little doubt that the
usual procedure was different.

Canyon de Chelly was occupied because it was the best place in that
vicinity for the practice of horticulture. The cliff ruins there grew out
of the natural conditions, as they have in other places. It is not meant
that a type of house structure developed here and was transferred
subsequently to other places. When the geological and topographical
environment favored their construction, cliff outlooks were built; from
a different geological structure in certain regions cavate lodges resulted;
in other places there were "watch towers;" in still others single rooms
were built, either alone or in clusters, and these results obtained quite
as often if not oftener within the historic period as in prehistoric times.

Notwithstanding the possible division of the De Chelly ruins into
four well defined types, there is no warrant for the assumption of a
large population. The types are interrelated and to a large extent
were inhabited not contemporaneously but conjointly. There are
about 140 ruins in Canyon de Chelly and its branches, but few of them
could accommodate more than a very small population. Settlements
large enough to furnish homes for 50 or 60 people were rare. As not
all of the sites were occupied at one time, the maximum population of
the canyon could hardly have exceeded 400; it is more likely to have
been 300.

The character of the site occupied is one of the most important elements to be studied in the examination of ruins in the pueblo country.
In De Chelly whatever defensive value the settlements had was due to
the character of the sites selected. It is believed, however, that other
considerations dictated the selection of the sites, and that the defensive
motive, if present at all, exercised very little influence in this region.
The sites here are always selected with a view to an outlook over some
adjacent area of cultivable land, and the structures erected on them
were industrial or horticultural, rather than military or defensive.

The masonry of the ruins and the constructive expedients employed by the builders are an insurmountable obstacle in the way of the hypothesis that the cliff ruins represent a primitive or intermediate stage in the growth of pueblo architecture. The builders were well acquainted with the principles and methods of construction employed in the best work found in other regions; the inferiority of their work is due to special conditions and to the locality. The presence of a number of extraneous features, both in methods and principles employed, is further evidence in the same line. These features are certainly foreign to this region, some of them suggest even Spanish or Mexican origin, which implies comparatively recent occupancy.

The openings—doorways and windows—found in the ruins are of the regular pueblo types. They are arranged as convenience dictated, without any reference to the defensive motive, which, if it existed at all, exercised less influence here than it did in the modern pueblos. There is no evidence of the use of very modern features, such as the paneled wooden doors found in the pueblos; nor, on the other hand, are there any very primitive expedients or methods—none which can not be found today in the modern villages.

The roof, floors, and timber work are also essentially the same as the examples found in the modern pueblos. The notable scarcity of roofing timbers in the ruins can probably be explained by the hypothesis of successive occupancies and subsequent or repeated use of material difficult to obtain. So far as regards the use of timber as an element of masonry construction the results obtained in De Chelly are rude and primitive as compared with the work found in other regions.

The immense number of storage cists found in De Chelly are a natural outgrowth of the conditions there and support the hypothesis that the cliff outlooks were merely farming shelters. The small size of many of the settlements made the construction of storage cists a necessity. The storage of water was very seldom attempted. A large proportion of the cists found in De Chelly were burial places and of Navaho origin. As a rule they are far more difficult of access than the ruins.

There is no evidence of the influence of the defensive motive. Defensive works on the approaches to sites are never found, nor can such influence be detected in the arrangement of openings, in the character of masonry, or in the ground plan. If the cliff ruins were defensive structures, an influence strong enough to bring about the occupancy of such inconvenient and unsuitable sites would certainly be strong enough also to bring about some slight modifications in the architecture, such as would render more suitable sites available. If we assume that the cliff ruins were farming outlooks, occupied only during the farming season, and then only for a few days or weeks at a time, the character of the sites occupied by them seems natural enough, for the same sites are used by the Navaho today in connection with farming operations.

The distribution of kivas in the ruins of De Chelly affords another indication that the occupancy of that region was quiet and little disturbed, and that the ruins were in no sense defensive structures. Kivas are found only in permanent settlements, and the presence of two or three of them in a small settlement comprising a total of five or six rooms implies, first, that the little village was the home of two or more families, and, second, that there was comparative if not entire immunity from hostile incursions. If the conditions were otherwise, these small settlements would have combined into larger ones, as was done in other regions. Probably these small settlements with several kivas mark a late period in the use of outlying sites. The position of the kivas in some of the settlements on defensive sites, and their arrangement across the front of the cove, suggest that such sites were first used for outlooks, and that their occupancy by regular villages came at a later period.

All of the now available traditions of the Navaho and of the Hopi Indians support the conclusions reached from a study of the intrinsic evidence of the ruins, that they represent a comparatively late period in the history of pueblo architecture. It appears that some at least of the ruins are of Hopi origin. It is certain that the ruins were not occupied at one time, nor by one tribe or band.

As criteria in development or in time the cliff ruins are valueless, except in a certain restricted way. They represent simply a phase of pueblo life, due more to the geological character of the region occupied than to extraordinary conditions, and they pertain partly to the old villages, partly to the more modern. Apparently they reached their greatest (not their highest) development in the period immediately preceding the last well-defined stage in the growth of pueblo architecture, a stage in which most of the pueblos were at the time of their discovery by the Spaniards, and in which some of them are now. Reliance for defense was had on the site occupied, and outlying settlements for horticultural purposes were very numerous, as they must necessarily be also in the last stage—the aggregation of many related villages into one great cluster.

The cliff outlooks in Canyon de Chelly and in other regions, the cavate lodges of New Mexico and Arizona, the "watch towers" of the San Juan and of the Zuñi country, the summer villages attached to many of the pueblos, the single-room remains found everywhere, even the brush shelters or "kisis" of Tusayan, are all functionally analogous, and all are the outgrowth of certain industrial requirements, which were essentially the same throughout the pueblo country, but whose product was modified by geological and topographical conditions. In the cliff ruins of De Chelly we have an interesting and most instructive example of the influence of a peculiar and sometimes adverse environment on a primitive people, who entered the region with preconceived and, as it were, fully developed ideas of house construction, and who left it before those ideas were brought fully in accord with the environment, but not before they were influenced by it.